# FIRE IN THE BELLY

The inside story of
the modern Olympics

1904 St
of th
Engl

France
1924 Paris,
The Ga

192

T

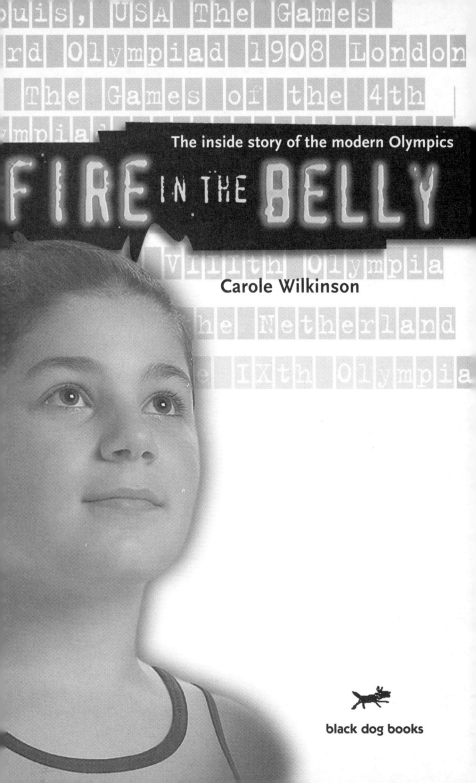

The inside story of the modern Olympics

# FIRE IN THE BELLY

Carole Wilkinson

black dog books

First published in 2004 by

black dog books
15 Gertrude Street
Fitzroy Vic 3065
Australia
61 + 3 + 9419 9406
61 + 3 + 9419 1214 (fax)
dog@bdb.com.au
www.bdb.com.au

Carole Wilkinson asserts the moral right to be identified
as author of this Work.

Copyright © Carole Wilkinson 2004

First published 2004

All rights reserved. Apart from any fair dealing for the purposes of
study, research, criticism or review, as permitted under the Copyright
Act, no part of this book may be reproduced by any process, stored in a
retrieval system, or transmitted in any form, without permission of the
copyright owner. All inquiries should be made to the publisher at the
address above.

Designed by Karen Young
Cover photographs: John Brash (girl in foreground), Hulton Archive
(lower background), PhotoDisc (upper background)
Printed and bound by Griffin Press

National Library of Australia
Cataloguing-in-Publication data:

       Wilkinson, Carole, 1950- .
       Fire in the belly : the inside story of the modern Olympics.

       Bibliography.
       Includes index.
       For children.
       ISBN 1 876372 47 8.

       1. Olympics - History.  I. Title.

796.48

# CONTENTS

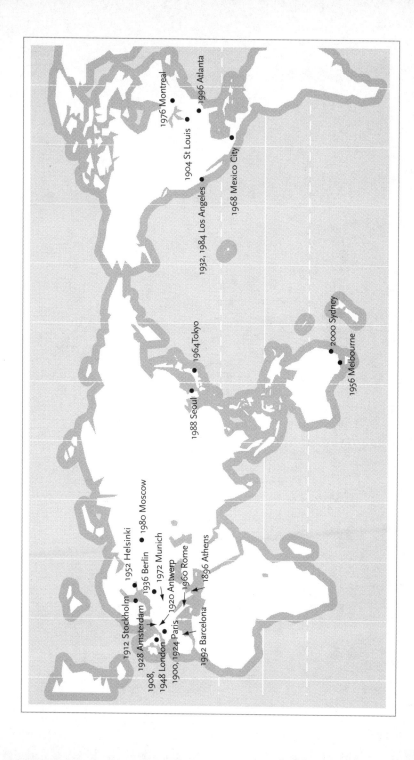

1976 Montreal
1996 Atlanta
1904 St Louis
1968 Mexico City
1932, 1984 Los Angeles

2000 Sydney
1956 Melbourne

1964 Tokyo
1988 Seoul

1952 Helsinki
1980 Moscow
1936 Berlin
1972 Munich
1920 Antwerp
1960 Rome
1896 Athens
1912 Stockholm
1928 Amsterdam
1908, 1948 London
1900, 1924 Paris
1992 Barcelona

## Symbols

| | |
|---|---|
|  | Year |
| | City |
| | Country |
| | Number of countries taking part |
| | Number of sports in competition |
| | Number of male athletes attending |
| | Number of female athletes attending |
| | Countries that won most medals: 1st, 2nd and 3rd placings |

*We shall not have peace until the prejudices which now separate the different races shall have been outlived. To attain this end, what better means than to bring the youth of all countries periodically together for amicable trials of muscular strength and agility?*

**Baron de Coubertin**, IOC President 1896–1925

# OUT OF THE PAST

In ancient Greece, a festival to honour the god Zeus was held every four years. The festivities included a sporting event held at a place called Olympia. Olympia wasn't a town, but an area where the gods were worshipped. As well as temples there was also a stadium where the sporting contests were held, a gymnasium where athletes practised throwing the discus and the javelin, an arena where wrestlers and boxers learned their skills, and a place called a hippodrome for chariot races.

The ancient Olympic Games were held from 776 BCE until 329 CE when the Romans banned the Games because they were un-Christian. Fire and foreign invaders then reduced Olympia to ruins. Floods, landslides and two earthquakes rearranged the landscape, burying all trace of the lovely buildings.

## Unearthed

In 1875, more than a thousand years later, a team of German archeologists began excavating the site of Olympia. The altar to Zeus and the ruins of the ancient stadium were unearthed.

In France, a man called Baron Pierre de Coubertin read a newspaper article about the excavations at the site of the ancient Olympic Games. The Baron was a keen sportsman himself. His family was very wealthy, so he had plenty of time to indulge in his favourite sports—boxing, fencing and horse-riding. He believed that sporting activity was not only the way to a healthy body, but also to a healthy mind. Every young person should take part in sport, he believed.

Reading about the excavations at Olympia gave him a brilliant idea. What the world needed was a modern Olympic Games. They would encourage people to take up sport. These Games wouldn't just be open to Greeks—they would be open to the whole world, bringing nations together in peace and harmony. He invited important people from different countries to a meeting and told them about his plan. They agreed that it was a good idea and formed the International Olympic Committee (IOC). Baron de Coubertin began to prepare for the first Olympic Games in 1500 years.

The statue of Zeus which stood in the temple at Olympia was one of the Seven Wonders of the Ancient World. It was made of gold, ivory and precious stones and stood 13 metres high (42 feet), as tall as a four-storey building.

The modern Olympic Games started in a small way with just 241 athletes taking part. If Baron de Coubertin was alive now, he would barely recognise the Games of today with more than 10 000 athletes taking part and millions of people all around the world watching the events on television.

The first thing competitors at an ancient Olympic Games had to do was pull up all the weeds that had grown in the stadium since the last Games.

## Big Issues

Over the history of the Games things have changed. Sporting methods and training techniques have evolved. New sports have been introduced while others have disappeared. Sportswomen have had to fight for their right to compete in the Olympics. The technology used for timing races, measuring jumps and bringing the Games to the world have all changed. The IOC has had to decide whether professional athletes should be allowed to take part. It has also had to decide what to do about athletes who take performance-enhancing drugs.

## People and Politics

World politics have found their way into the sports arena. With millions of people around the world watching, many people have used the Olympic Games to push issues into the world spotlight. Governments have used them to promote their views. Demonstrators and terrorists have forced their beliefs on the world via the Games. As athletes from all over the world competed on the sports field, racial equality and campaigns for political freedom were publicised.

Every four years the world's attention turns to this one international event. As we cheer our sporting heroes, the current state of the world is brought into focus. Whether the Baron intended it or not, the Olympic Games have become much more than a sporting event.

# 1 FROM THE FIRST TO THE WORST

## Bay of Zea, Piraeus, 30 May 1896

*"The race will be cancelled, won't it?" asked my countryman. He was blue with cold.*

*We were both still shivering from our brief dip in the sea during the 100-metre swim (which I am proud to say I won).*

*"Of course," I replied as I watched huge waves crash on the beach, the foam carried off by a raging wind.*

*I was wrong. An official put a megaphone to his lips and announced that the race would start in 15 minutes.*

*My friend held out a jar of mutton fat.*

*"I've already covered myself with grease," I said. (I suspect that's why the other contestants were standing at a distance.)*

*"Put on more," he replied. "You'll need it."*

*Indeed, the weather had worsened. The wind was snapping the flags on the royal platform and the waves were as high as a house. My country, Hungary, has no coastline. Before today I had never swum in the sea. I dipped my fingers into the smelly grease and plastered it over my body until it was a good centimetre thick.*

"Good luck, Alfred," my friend said. He had decided not to compete in this race. I was beginning to think I should follow his example.

I walked with the other shivering competitors up the jetty, past the royal platform towards a small boat. I had thought we would swim across the bay, but the officials had another plan. We climbed into the boat and were swiftly carried away from the shore. The boat rose over each gigantic wave, plunging down on the other side only to be raised up again. We were taken more than a kilometre out to sea. I am no sailor. Even after such a short trip I was feeling sick.

A strange sight appeared before us—a row of orange pumpkin gourds strung together bobbing up and down in the water. It took me a moment or two to realise that this was the starting line. The pumpkins looked very festive, like a string of decorations. I didn't feel festive at all. I felt terrified.

I shuddered in the freezing wind and reminded myself I was doing this for the glory of my country. I hummed the Hungarian anthem to encourage me. Without warning there was the crack of gunfire and the other swimmers leapt over the side of the boat. I hesitated, but an official, thinking I hadn't heard the starting pistol, pushed me into the sea. It was like falling into a bath of ice. The freezing water drew the breath from me. I was thinking that I would pull out of the race, when the boat sped off back to the shore.

All I could see were huge grey waves, surging around me in every direction. Here and there I glimpsed other stunned swimmers, struggling to stay afloat. The desire to bring glory *to my homeland was whisked away on the wind. I forgot about winning the race. I had only one thought. I had to get back to shore or I would die.*

*I started to swim, leaving my fellow competitors struggling in the waves. I struck out with my frozen arms. My body ached from head to foot with the cold. I had difficulty drawing breath. I couldn't see the beach or the jetty but I made sure that I swam with the breaking waves. I nearly collided with another swimmer who had given himself up to the mercy of the sea. He was being tossed about by the cruel waves. His eyes stared at me like those of a dying fish as I swam past him. That would be my fate if I didn't keep going.*

*At last I could make out the beach and the buildings of the town. I pushed harder. I wasn't going to die! I swam until my arms dug into sand, then I splashed ashore and threw myself gratefully onto the beach.*

*It was only then that I realised the crash of the waves on the beach had given way to another sound—loud cheering. The band was striking up a familiar tune. It was the Hungarian national anthem.*

*I looked up. My friend was running towards me with a blanket in his arms and a smile on his face.*

*"You won!" he shouted.*

**Alfréd Hajós**, Hungarian Olympic swimmer

It's difficult to imagine an Olympic swimming event taking place in the sea, but that's what happened at the first Olympics. There were a lot of things in the early Games that were different to the efficient spectacle that we see today.

# 1896 | ATHENS, GREECE
## *The Games of the I<sup>st</sup> Olympiad*

| | | | | | | | 1 | 2 | 3 |
|---|---|---|---|---|---|---|---|---|---|
| 1896 | Athens | Greece | 14 | 9 | 241 | 0 | Greece | USA | Germany |

Baron de Coubertin thought the first modern Olympic Games had to be in Greece. It wasn't possible to hold them among the ruins of Olympia, so Athens was chosen as the host city. To highlight Greece's ancient connection to the Olympic Games, an ancient stadium in Athens was used. The Panathenaic Stadium was first built in 330 BCE. It is a horseshoe-shaped, open-air stadium. It was restored, complete with white marble seats, for the first Games.

## The First Games

In the first modern Olympic Games only 14 countries competed, most of them European nations. America and Australia also had competitors, but they did not send official teams. Some of the competitors were people who happened to be in Europe on holiday at the time.

The Australian "team" was just one person, a runner called Edwin Flack, who was in London on a working holiday and decided he'd like to compete in the Olympic Games.

There were 43 sporting events—in athletics, swimming,

gymnastics, shooting, cycling, tennis, weightlifting and wrestling.

## Fanfare

Many of the symbols and ceremonies that we associate with the Olympic Games weren't a part of the early Games. In 1896 there was no lavish Opening Ceremony, there was no Olympic flame or torch relay, the flag with its five rings hadn't been designed. These things all came later.

There weren't even any gold medals. The winner of each event was given a silver medal, and a wreath of olive leaves was placed on his head. The runners-up each received a bronze medal and a laurel wreath.

From the very beginning, the public had a great interest in the Olympics. When the first Games opened, 40 000 spectators filled the stadium. Many more watched from the surrounding hills. The Crown Prince of Greece made a speech (this was before loud speakers were invented so not many people heard it!). The King proclaimed the Games open. A choir sang an Olympic hymn which had been written for the occasion. The packed stadium liked the hymn so much they demanded an encore. A flock of pigeons soared into the air symbolising peace and freedom. The release of pigeons or doves became a permanent part of Olympic ceremony.

## Calendar Confusion

There was something else that was different at the first Olympics—the calendar. Back in 1896, Greece was using a different calendar to most of the rest of the world. The

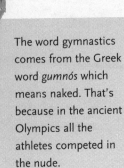

The word gymnastics comes from the Greek word *gumnós* which means naked. That's because in the ancient Olympics all the athletes competed in the nude.

calendar we use today is called the Gregorian Calendar. The Greeks were using the Julian Calendar which was 12 days in front.

The American team consisted of various college students who had decided they wanted to take part in the Games. There was no air travel back then. The only way to get overseas was by ship. The American students sailed on a cargo ship to Italy. They planned on arriving in Athens 12 days before the start of the Games so they had time to practise and get used to the venues.

When they arrived in Italy, someone told them about the different Greek calendar. They rushed to Greece—a trip that involved a dash across Italy, a ferry to Greece and then a 10-hour train journey to Athens. The American athletes arrived exhausted the night before the first events. They might have been tired, but they were ready to compete.

## First Olympian

The Greek spectators were very proud that their country was the home of the Olympic Games. They wanted their athletes to excel. They were disappointed that the first medal wasn't won by a Greek.

US triple jumper James Connolly became the first Olympic champion in 1500 years. The local crowd then watched as the Americans won medal after medal in the track and field events.

Discus throwing had been a popular sport in Greece for

more than 3000 years. The crowd was sure that a Greek would win this event, but the Americans won again. Bob Garrett had never seen a discus when he started training for the event back in America. He got a friend to make him a discus to practise with. When he arrived

French runner Albin Lermusiaux ran wearing white gloves because the race was being watched by royalty.

in Greece he discovered that his homemade discus was much heavier than the real thing. He threw the lighter discus and easily beat the Greek champion.

In fact the only athletics events the Americans didn't win were the two won by the lone Australian.

## Main Event

When Baron de Coubertin was planning the Olympic Games, he wanted there to be a showcase event, a symbolic link to the ancient Games. There was a legend that in 490 BCE a Greek messenger by the name of Phiedippides had run all the way from the Plain of Marathon to Athens. He delivered the news that the Greeks had won a battle against the Persians. Even though the messenger dropped dead of exhaustion when he arrived, the Olympic organisers thought it would be a wonderful idea to have a race from Marathon to the Olympic stadium in Athens—a distance of about 40 kilometres (25 miles).

On the day of the marathon race, the stadium was packed. The spectators were hoping that a Greek runner would save Greek pride and win the marathon. They waited patiently to see who would arrive first. In those days there was no television. There wasn't even a radio

*"When Loues entered the Stadion, the crowd, which numbered sixty thousand persons, rose to its feet like one man, swayed with extraordinary excitement...A flight of white pigeons was let loose, women waved fans and handkerchiefs..."*
**Baron de Coubertin**,
IOC President
1896–1925

broadcast to give them a clue as to who was in front. The only news came via a messenger on horseback.

Most competitors weren't used to such a long distance. Many gave up or collapsed along the way. As the remaining runners got closer, news spread by word of mouth—a Greek runner was in the lead. As he entered the stadium, the crowd cheered wildly. The two Greek princes climbed down from their velvet-cushioned seats to run at his side.

But who was the winner? It turned out to be a soldier called Spiridon Loues. Before he joined the army he was an unknown shepherd from a small village. Now he had become a Greek national hero.

## Youngest Olympian

Another Greek whose name has gone into the sporting history books is a gymnast named Dimitrios Loundras. He was only 10 years old when he came third in the team parallel bars event. He didn't actually win a medal as medals were only given to first and second place-getters in 1896, but the IOC lists him as a bronze medallist because he came in third place. As well as coming third, he was also last as there were only three teams competing!

## Men Only

The ancient Olympic Games had only been open to free

Greek men. Women and slaves could not compete. In fact, women weren't allowed to watch and were threatened with death if they even entered the stadium.

Baron de Coubertin, just like the ancient Greeks, thought that women shouldn't compete in the modern Olympic games. It was okay for young girls to undertake gentle exercise in private, but he thought it was very unfeminine for grown women to be seen in public running and jumping...and sweating. Some doctors believed women were too weak for such heavy exercise and it would be bad for their health.

The Baron did allow women into the stadium, but he thought that the only place for women at the Olympics was applauding the male athletes. It wasn't long before female athletes were fighting to compete in the Olympic Games.

# 1900 PARIS, FRANCE
### *The Games of the II<sup>nd</sup> Olympiad*

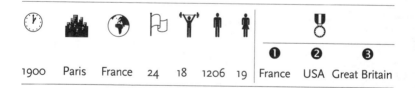

| | | | | | | | 1 | 2 | 3 |
|---|---|---|---|---|---|---|---|---|---|
| 1900 | Paris | France | 24 | 18 | 1206 | 19 | France | USA | Great Britain |

The Greek people thought they had the right to host every Olympic Games, just as they had in ancient times. Baron de Coubertin had other ideas. He wanted the Games to be like the ancient Games in most ways—they were to be held every four years, no professional sportsmen could take part, and there certainly weren't going to be any women! But if the Games were going to help bring world peace, he believed they had to be held in a different country each time. He decided that Paris, his home town, would be the next city to host the modern Olympic Games.

## The Invisible Games

The Baron had grand plans for the 1900 Olympics. He wanted to build a replica of Olympia, just as it had been at the ancient Games. He made a big mistake though. Instead of having the Games as a stand-alone event, he made them part of the International Exhibition which was already scheduled to be held in Paris. In the end no new venues were built for the Olympics. The swimming events took place in the dirty River Seine; the track and field events in a park called the Bois du Boulogne. It was very scenic, but the runners had to run on a bumpy grass track instead of a cinder track. Old telephone poles were used as hurdles. Athletes lost discuses and javelins in the trees.

At the 1900 Olympics, sporting events were attached to different sections of the International Exhibition—fencing and skating (perhaps because they involved sharp blades) became part of the cutlery exhibit!

The Olympic events were spread over five months and buried among the other events at the Exhibition. The 1900 Olympic Games were bigger, but they weren't better.

## Exhibitions

The Baron and the IOC were left out

of the planning process. The organisers of the International Exhibition made up their own rules. They didn't even call it the Olympic Games and they held some very un-Olympic events. Ballooning was on the program. So was automobile racing and fishing. In swimming there was an obstacle race, where the competitors had to swim under and clamber over boats.

The marathon was not the exciting spectacle it had been in 1896. Spectators got in the runners' way and the winner may well have won because he took a shortcut. The Games were so disorganised that some athletes missed their events. Many athletes didn't even know they were taking part in the Olympic Games. Some didn't find out until years later.

## The Human Frog

There were still highlights at the 1900 Olympics. One exceptional athlete was American Ray Ewry, an expert at the standing jumps—the standing high jump, the standing long jump and the standing triple jump. These events involved jumping from a standing position without a run-up. Ray Ewry won gold medals in all three events.

His achievements were even more amazing because, when he was a child, he'd had a disease called polio. His legs were paralysed and doctors told him he would spend his life in a wheelchair. Ray wouldn't accept this and he began a strict exercise regime. Not only did he walk again, his legs became exceptionally strong. At the 1900 Games he jumped 3.3 metres (10 feet 10 inches) in the long jump and 1.6 metres (5 feet 3 inches) in the high jump. The French spectators were so impressed they called him the Human Frog.

The standing jumps were dropped from the Olympics in 1912.

## Mystery Olympian

The Dutch rowing team didn't have a cox for the coxed pairs race. A cox or coxswain is someone who sits at the back of the boat encouraging the crew, steering the boat and shouting instructions at the rowers. These instructions help the rowers (who are facing the back of the boat) row straight and improve their rowing technique during a race. A small person is usually chosen to be the cox so that they add as little extra weight as possible.

The Dutch rowers asked a young French boy to be their cox. To their delight the Dutch pair won the race. The French cox had his photograph taken with the winners and then went home. No one thought to ask him his name.

The mystery cox might be the youngest Olympian ever, but his exact age when he competed isn't known.

## Enter the Ladies

The chaos and confusion of the 1900 Olympics was a good thing for one group of athletes. Five countries sent women competitors to the Games. With the Baron out of the picture, no one objected. Women competed in golf, tennis, croquet, yachting and equestrian events. They had managed to get into the Olympics and they were there to stay.

Charlotte Cooper, British tennis player and Wimbledon

champion, is usually mentioned as being the first ever female Olympic medallist. But researchers have discovered that there was a woman among one of the Swiss yachting crews. She was Helen, Countess de Pourtalès and she was the

In the 1900s, women played tennis in ankle-length skirts.

first woman to receive an Olympic medal. Charlotte remains the first individual female medallist.

The Baron never changed his opinion about women in sport. Years later he still referred to women's involvement in the Olympics as a "regrettable impurity".

The idea of women wearing bathing suits and shorts in public was still too shocking to consider. Women had to wait a while before they could compete in athletics and swimming.

# 1904 ST LOUIS, USA
## *The Games of the III$^{rd}$ Olympiad*

| ⏱ | 🏙 | 🌍 | 🏳 | 🏋 | 👨 | 👩 | 🎖 | | |
|---|---|---|---|---|---|---|---|---|---|
| | | | | | | | **❶** | **❷** | **❸** |
| 1904 | St Louis | USA | 13 | 17 | 681 | 8 | USA | Germany | Canada |

The next Olympic Games were to be held in St Louis in the USA. Unfortunately there was another International Exhibition being held there at the same time. It included

US athlete George Eyser was one of the most amazing gymnasts ever. He won six medals at the 1904 Olympic Games even though he had a wooden leg.

international sporting events. The Baron was worried that having two competing sporting events would be disastrous. You'd think that after the Paris Games, the Baron would have learned his lesson, but he hadn't. He decided to allow the 1904 Olympic Games to be part of the International Exhibition. The Olympics went from bad to worse.

## The Worst Games

The 1904 Olympic Games were not well attended—by athletes or by spectators. Even Baron de Coubertin didn't bother to go. Nothing illustrates the disastrous St Louis Games better than the marathon.

The race was run in terrible conditions. It was a hot day and the chosen route consisted of dusty, rutted dirt roads. There was only one water stop for the competitors. One runner was chased from the course by dogs, another was found unconscious by the side of the road. Cuban runner, Félix Carvajal de Soto, however, found the time to chat to spectators and to steal apples from an orchard.

## Marathon Mess

The first marathon runner to return to the stadium was American Fred Lorz. He didn't appear at all exhausted as he ran across the finishing line. The second runner, Tom Hicks, another American, staggered into the stadium, stumbled over the line and collapsed. Just as Fred was being handed his gold medal, he confessed that he'd actually taken a lift in a car for part of the race! He said it was meant to be a joke, but officials were not amused. The gold medal was then awarded to Tom Hicks.

The reason for Tom's wavering entrance to the stadium was soon discovered. During the race he had been close to collapse. He wanted to give up, but his trainers gave him strychnine. This is a deadly poison in high doses, but a small amount acts as a stimulant. Throughout the race he was given more strychnine and brandy. There were no rules about drug use in sport back then, so Tom Hicks is still recorded as the winner. Stopping Olympic athletes from using drugs became the goal of the IOC in later years and is still a major issue today.

## Sideshow

If that wasn't bad enough, there was another event at St Louis which was even more disgraceful. It was called Anthropology Days. It consisted of competitions between so-called "primitive" races of the world such as American Indians, Asians and black Africans. The whole purpose was to show the superiority of "civilised" white athletes over these people who had never taken part in sporting events before. It was the lowest point of the Olympic Games.

When Baron de Coubertin heard about Anthropology Days, he was horrified. He said that once people from other races had proper training in sport, they would become successful athletes. This turned out to be a very accurate prediction. Racial equality has been a theme underlying the Olympic Games ever since.

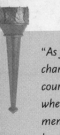

"As for that outrageous charade, it will of course lose its appeal when black men, red men and yellow men learn to run, jump, and throw and leave the white man far behind them."

**Baron de Coubertin,**
IOC President
1896–1925

The tone of the 1904 Olympics is illustrated by George Lyon, a Canadian golfer, who walked on his hands to the podium to collect his medal. The Olympic Games had turned into a laughable sideshow. It looked like the end of the Olympic Movement.

# 2 | REVIVAL

## Windsor Castle, 30 May 1908

*The Olympic Games opened with a fanfare of trumpets. The band of the Grenadier Guards played 'God Save the King'.*

"Will Your Majesty graciously declare the fourth Olympiad open?" asked Lord Desborough (he's the head of the British Olympic Committee).

"I declare the London Games open," Grandpapa replied.

Then all the contestants from all the nations entered the stadium, each behind their country's flag. At least I believe that's what happened. I didn't see it myself. Mama and Papa told me all about it. They went in a horse-drawn carriage. I had to stay at Windsor with my brothers. Being a princess has no advantage at all.

I asked Papa if, since I missed the opening ceremonies, I could see some of the races. After all it isn't every day that the Olympic Games are held in one's own country. England may never hold the Games again, I told him, it might be my last chance. He took no notice. I will not see a single race.

"You'd be sitting in the rain," Nanny said. "Why would

you want to do that? You're better off staying here at Windsor Castle."

*It's not fair. Nobody is on my side.*

*Mama will start the marathon. The race should be 25 miles long, the distance from Marathon to Athens, but Mama has requested that the race start from here at Windsor Castle, so that she can start the race without having to go all the way to London again. That means the race will now be 26 miles from here to the Royal Box at the stadium.*

"Then I can see the start!" I said to Papa.

"No, no," he replied. "If you are there, the princes will want to be there as well. They'll just get in the way."

*It's very vexing. I'm sure if Edward or George wanted to see the start of the marathon they'd be allowed to.*

"If I lean out of the window I should be able to see it," I told Nanny, but she said she would bolt all the windows, as it would be her fault if I fell out and broke my neck.

*I had an idea. Last week I got Edward to help me measure the distance from the nursery to the gate where the race is to start. His stride is about a yard. It was 385 yards.*

Lord Desborough came down to Windsor to talk over the arrangements with Mama that same day. I managed to slip away from Nanny and found them in the Picture Gallery.

"Good morning, Your Highness," he said.

I didn't waste time on pleasantries. I knew that Nanny would be after me and make me go back to the nursery.

"Lord Desborough," I said. "If the Olympic marathon can

be made a mile longer to suit Mama, can't it be made another 385 yards longer?"

"What would be the point of that?" he asked, somewhat puzzled by my question.

"That way the marathon could start at the East Terrace beneath the nursery window and then I could see the start without having to go outdoors."

He didn't look convinced that this was a good idea.

"The princes would be thrilled," I added. The boys always get whatever they want.

"I'm sure something can be arranged," replied Lord Desborough with a smile.

Mama was very cross that I had interrupted her meeting.

I thought that I had heard the end of it, until today. Today I found out that Lord Desborough has kept his word. The Olympic marathon is to start on the East Terrace! Runners from all nations, 75 of them, will line up beneath our window. Just this once the marathon will be 26 miles 385 yards long.

**Princess Mary,** Granddaughter of King Edward VII, aged 11

The princess got her wish, and the marathon of the 1908 Olympic Games started outside the nursery window at Windsor Castle. Strangely enough, the length of the marathon didn't go back to being 25 miles in the following Olympic Games. In fact the Olympic marathon is still 26 miles and 385 yards (or 42.195 km) to this day.

# 1908

| 1908 | London | England | 22 | 22 | 1999 | 36 | Great Britain | USA | Sweden |
| --- | --- | --- | --- | --- | --- | --- | --- | --- | --- |
| | | | | | | | ❶ | ❷ | ❸ |

Baron de Coubertin knew that if the next Olympic Games weren't a success, it would be the end of the Olympic Movement. This time he made sure that he kept a firm control of them.

London was chosen as the next host city. The organisers built a new stadium which contained not only an athletics track, but also a cycling track, football pitch, gymnastics platform and an enormous 100-metre (328-foot) swimming pool. For the first time the Olympic Games began to take on the form that we are familiar with today. There was an Opening Ceremony where all national teams marched into the stadium behind their country's flag.

## The Fiery Games

In 1908, the relationship between America and Britain was not good. This unfriendliness spilled out onto the athletics track. It all started when the American team marched into the stadium during the Opening Ceremony. The flags of all the participating nations were flying around the stadium.

The Americans looked for their flag. It was missing. They were deeply offended.

It had been agreed that as the flag-bearer for each country passed the royal box, they would dip their flag in honour of the King of England. The US flag-bearer, champion shot putter Ralph Rose, decided that if the British were going to be disrespectful, so would the Americans. He marched by the royal box without dipping the flag.

This was the first time that the Olympics had been used to express political opinions. It wasn't the last.

## Objections

That was only the beginning. The Americans were convinced that the British officials favoured British athletes, and they objected to judges' decisions on a daily basis.

Tug of war sounds like a kids' game today, but it was a serious Olympic sport from 1900–1920. The Americans complained that the British tug of war team was wearing illegal footwear and pulled out of the contest.

In the final of the 400-metre race there were four runners—three Americans and one British. An American runner was accused of deliberately cutting off the British runner. The judges declared

One strange sport held at the 1908 Olympics was bicycle polo. It was a demonstration sport and no medals were awarded. Australian rules football, roller hockey and pelota basque (a ball game played with a wicker basket strapped to the player's wrist and used as a racquet) were demonstration sports held at other Olympics.

the race void. The Americans refused to take part in a rerun. The British runner ran the race alone and, of course, won the gold medal.

## More Marathon Drama

Once again the marathon was a source of controversy. The first runner to enter the stadium was Italian Dorando Pietri. Exhausted and disorientated, he staggered in the wrong direction and collapsed. Officials helped him to his feet, pointed him in the right direction and he stumbled on. He collapsed another four times and officials helped him as he fell over the finishing line. The second runner, American Johnny Hayes, ran to the finishing line unaided…and complained that Pietri wouldn't have made it without the help of the British officials. Pietri was disqualified and Hayes won the gold medal.

## Olympic Power

The Olympic Games was back in the control of the IOC, but who were these people who made the decisions?

The first IOC consisted of 14 rich, European men— members of royal families, millionaires and businessmen. They were hand-picked by Baron de Coubertin and they all had similar views to him. In reality, the Baron pretty much got his own way on everything.

Over the years, the IOC has become a powerful body dealing with billions of dollars.

## Success

Among the controversies in 1908, there were sporting

triumphs. Many swimming world records were broken as the races were held in a pool for the first time (instead of the sea, a lake or a dirty river as in previous Olympics). Ray Ewry, in his final Games, won more gold medals in the standing jumps, bringing his total to eight gold. This is still the most gold medals any Olympic athlete has ever won in individual events.

It was reported that one of the officials who helped the Italian runner in the 1908 Marathon was Sir Arthur Conan Doyle, creator of Sherlock Holmes.

Overall the 1908 Games were a huge success. Many people think that if it hadn't been for this success, the Olympic Games would never have continued.

# 1912 STOCKHOLM, SWEDEN
## *The Games of the V<sup>th</sup> Olympiad*

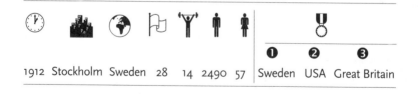

| 🕐 | 🏙 | 🌍 | 🏳 | 🏋 | 🧍 | 🧍 | 🏅 | | |
| --- | --- | --- | --- | --- | --- | --- | --- | --- | --- |
| | | | | | | | ❶ | ❷ | ❸ |
| 1912 | Stockholm | Sweden | 28 | 14 | 2490 | 57 | Sweden | USA | Great Britain |

The Olympic Games held in Sweden in 1912 went almost without a hitch. At last the world was starting to treat the Games with the respect and importance that Baron de Coubertin had dreamed of. Twenty-eight nations sent teams, including Japan which was the first Asian country to take part. After the claims of biased judging in London, a team of international referees was selected to judge the events.

## The Efficient Games

As well as providing excellent facilities and well-organised operation, the Swedish Olympic Committee also introduced some technical innovations. They used electrical devices which timed races to a 10th of a second. Photographs were taken at the finishing line to help decide close finishes. For the first time everyone in the stadium could hear announcements and speeches, thanks to the use of a public address system.

## Pentathlon x2

A sport from the ancient Games was included in the Olympic program in 1912. It was the pentathlon which involved five different athletic events—long jump, discus throwing, javelin throwing, a 200-metre race and a 1500-metre race.

In 1912, Baron de Coubertin also introduced another pentathlon which he invented himself. He called it the modern pentathlon. The Baron was inspired by the deeds of a 19th century French cavalry officer who had to ride through enemy lines to deliver a message. Along the way he had a sword fight and had to shoot at enemy soldiers. Then his horse was shot so he had to swim across a river and run the rest of the way on foot. The modern pentathlon consists of riding, fencing, shooting, swimming and a cross-country run.

The ancient-style pentathlon was discontinued after 1924, but the modern pentathlon is still an Olympic event today.

## Stripped

The gold medal winner of the old-style pentathlon was Jim Thorpe. This part-Native American athlete was a crowd favourite even though he beat the Swedish athletes. He also easily won the other all-round Olympic contest, the decathlon (a 10-event sport), and established world records in both events. The King of Sweden was so impressed that he gave Jim a bronze bust of himself. The Tsar of Russia presented him with a jewelled chalice. Back at home he was given a ticker-tape parade. But the following year someone discovered that Jim had earned $15 a week playing minor-league baseball. Earning money from playing sport was against Olympic rules. Jim was stripped of his gold medals and his Olympic career was over.

There was a campaign to reinstate Jim Thorpe into Olympic records and give him back his medals. The campaign was eventually successful. But Jim's supporters didn't win their battle until 1982—30 years after his death.

Swedish athletes won all three medals in the first modern pentathlon, but the fifth placed athlete was an American called George Patton. He didn't earn any fame from his athletic achievements, but during World War II he became famous as a general.

## Lethal Running

The 1912 marathon turned into a tragic event. The race

was held on a very hot day and included rough gravel tracks and steep hills. Half the runners didn't finish the race. The Portuguese runner Francisco Lazaro collapsed from sunstroke and heart problems. He was taken to hospital and died the next day. He was only 21 years old.

## Wrestling Marathon

It takes runners between two and three hours to run the marathon. At the 1912 Olympics there was a much longer event.

Greco-Roman wrestling sounds like an ancient sport, but it isn't. This style of wrestling was created in the 19th century, not in Greece or in Italy either, but in France. It has different rules to freestyle wrestling (also an Olympic sport)—only certain types of holds are allowed.

One of the semi-final bouts was between Estonian wrestler Martin Klein and Finnish wrestler Alfred Asikainen. There were no time limits for wrestling matches back then. The bout lasted for 11 hours and 40 minutes when Klein eventually won. He was so exhausted he couldn't take part in the final the next day. A Swedish wrestler won the final without having to wrestle anybody.

The ancient amateur athlete was a myth. Ancient Greek athletes received rewards for their efforts. In 2nd century BCE, professional Greek athletes belonged to athletic guilds similar to unions today.

## Amateur Versus Professional

The IOC had lost the battle to keep women out of the Olympics. In 1912 women competed officially for the first time, with 57 women competing in six events. But the IOC was determined to keep professionals out of the Olympics. Baron de Coubertin and later presidents of the IOC claimed that it was necessary to restrict the Olympics to amateurs. They only wanted competitors who played sport for honour in the Olympic Games. They didn't want anybody who did it to make money.

The IOC carried their beliefs to extremes. Australian swimmer Frank Beaurepaire wasn't allowed to compete in the 1912 Olympics because he worked as a physical education instructor. In 1936 American swimmer Eleanor Holm was warned that she could not compete in the Olympics if she played the part of a swimmer in a movie or earned money from modelling swimsuits.

Whether the IOC intended it or not, the amateur rule meant that the majority of Olympic competitors were rich white men. Most working-class athletes like Jim Thorpe couldn't afford to only play sport, they had to earn a living as well. Many of them earned it doing what they were good at—sport.

## Well-oiled Machine

The Olympic Games were running smoothly. They were popular with spectators and competitors alike. After a wobbly start they had become one of the most important sporting events in the world. Nothing could stand in the way of the Games getting bigger and better...or could it?

"Rules are like steam rollers. There is nothing they won't do to flatten the man who stands in their way."
**Jim Thorpe**, US Olympic track and field athlete

31

# 1920 | ANTWERP, BELGIUM
## Games of the VII<sup>th</sup> Olympiad

| 1920 | Antwerp Belgium | 29 | 22 | 2591 | 78 | ❶ USA | ❷ Sweden | ❸ Great Britain |
|------|-----------------|----|----|------|----|-------|----------|-----------------|

Just when the Olympic Games was becoming a well-organised event, something outside the control of the Baron and the IOC stopped it in its tracks. The 1916 Games were cancelled because of World War I. The war was over by the time the next Games were due, but it still affected the Olympics. The honour of hosting the Games was given to Antwerp. This was because the people of Belgium had suffered greatly during the war and Antwerp had been occupied by German troops.

## The Post-war Games

The Belgians did their best to build good venues for the Olympics, but there was no time or money to build spectacular stadiums so soon after the war. The athletes had to sleep in local schools on bunks with straw-filled pillows. The swimming pool looked impressive at first glance, but the water was dark and freezing cold. The divers wore socks and scarves between dives to try and keep warm.

The war affected the number of countries that took part in the Games as well. Germany and its allies—Austria, Hungary and Turkey—were not invited.

## Two Weeks in a Rusty Boat

The American male athletes sailed to Belgium on a rusty old ship that had been used to return the bodies of dead soldiers to the USA during the war. The athletes slept in the ship's hold and had rats for company. They protested, but it was too late to make any changes. There were no training facilities on board. The track and field athletes tied their javelins and discuses to the ship with rope so that they could throw them out to sea and then haul them back in.

## Fast Finnish

Since the first Olympics, the US had always dominated the track and field events, winning most of the medals. In 1920, Finland was competing as an independent country for the first time. This little country, with a population around a 40th of that of America, won nine gold medals in track and field—the same number as the United States. Long-distance runner Paavo Nurmi made his Olympic debut with three gold medals and one silver.

## Old Man of the Olympics

One of the heroes of the 1920 Olympics was a Swedish shooter called Oscar Swahn whose specialty was the running deer event. This was his third Olympic Games. At previous Games he had won two gold medals and three bronze medals. In 1920 he won a silver medal. What was so special about Oscar? He was 72 years old. He didn't even start competing in the Olympics until he was 60. He still holds the record for being the oldest Olympic medallist ever.

## Olympic Rings

In 1920 the Olympic flag made its first appearance. Baron de Coubertin designed the flag himself. The design consists of five interlocking coloured rings—blue, yellow, black, green and red—on a white background. It represents international harmony. Every country in the world has at least one of the colours in its flag. The flag was made in Paris and measured 3 metres by 2 metres (9 foot 6 inches by 6 foot 7 inches). The Olympic rings have become one of the most well-known symbols in the world.

Another Olympic tradition was introduced at the Antwerp Games—the athletes' oath. At the beginning of each Games one athlete from the host nation is chosen to recite an oath on behalf of all the athletes. The oath promises that the athletes will play by the rules in a fair and sportsmanlike way. In 1920, Belgian fencer and water polo player Victor Boin took the oath. He had been a pilot during the recent war. The words in the oath have been changed slightly to make them modern, but it is basically the same oath that is used today.

*We swear that we are taking part in the Olympic Games as loyal competitors, observing the rules governing the Games, and anxious to show a spirit of chivalry for the honour of our countries and for the glory of sport.*

**First Athletes' Oath**, 1920

## Financial Flop

Inviting Antwerp to host the 1920 Games was a noble gesture, but not a very wise one. Attendance was poor and the organisers made a loss. Sticking up posters was the main way of advertising an upcoming event back in 1920. After the war there was a shortage of paper which meant that the organising committee couldn't print many posters. Many people just didn't know that the Olympics were taking place. Tickets to see Olympic events were expensive and it rained for almost the whole Games. The war-weary Belgian people weren't that interested in the Olympics, they just wanted to get on with their lives.

*"These five rings represent the five parts of the world now won over to the Olympism ... Also the six colours thus combined represent those of all nations, with no exceptions. This is a real international emblem."*
**Baron de Coubertin**, IOC President 1896–1925

# 3

## FASTER, HIGHER, STRONGER

### Le Vélodrome d'Hiver, Paris, 30 June 1924

*I wasn't really paying much attention to the fencing match between the French and the Italians. It was the final of the foils competition which involves the use of a sword with a flexible blade and a blunt end. The object of the contest is to touch your opponent with the tip of the foil somewhere on the body between the collarbone and the hipbone and, of course, at the same time to prevent him from touching you. Fencing is an old and honourable sport.*

*I am the coach of the Hungarian Olympic fencing team. It is a great honour. My team had already finished their bout against the Argentinians. They had done very well, but they didn't have enough points for a medal. As I say I was only half watching the contest. The French team was leading 3–1. In this particular assault, a young Italian fencer by the name of Aldo Boni was tied with his French opponent at four touches each. Even if the Italian did win, as far as I was concerned, the French were on their way to a gold medal.*

*I was making some notes for one of my team, when I*

heard someone shouting in my native tongue. That got my attention. It seemed that the referee had awarded a fifth touch to the Frenchman and Boni was far from happy about it. The young Italian was shouting and shaking his fist at the referee.

The referee, as it happened, was a Hungarian man. He came over to me.

"You speak Italian don't you?" he asked (in Hungarian).

"Of course," I replied. "I was born in Italy."

"I'd be grateful if you would tell me what this young man is shouting about."

I could hardly refuse, but to be perfectly honest, what the young man was saying was very vulgar and offensive. It was certainly not the sort of language I would normally use, but I thought it my duty to translate what was said accurately. So I did. The referee was understandably offended.

"Tell him I demand an apology!" the referee shouted.

The hot-headed Boni wouldn't hear of it.

"I have nothing to apologise for!" he yelled back.

Before anyone had a chance to discuss it, the entire Italian team walked out as a protest, singing their anthem as they went.

Needless to say, the Italian team had to forfeit the rest of their matches. As a result the Italians came fourth and were denied a medal. Happily for my team, this gave us an unexpected bronze medal.

No reasonable person could blame me for this turn of events. Or so I thought. That was not the case though. Later, *a statement from the Italian Olympic fencing team was published. This declared that I had made up the insults the young Italian had flung at the referee because I wanted them to lose the match. This, it seems, was because I feared the Italians would beat my Hungarians.*

*I have stayed calm until now, but this is the final insult. I cannot sit by and let my name be dragged through the mud. I won't allow it.*

*All the members of my team have tried to talk me out of it. My son, Giorgio, has begged me not to go ahead, but I know what I must do. I have taken action this day. I have challenged the captain of the Italian team to a duel—not a sporting competition with blunt swords, you understand, but a real duel, using heavy sabres. Duels are now illegal here in France. Don't ask me why. It is the most civilised way to settle an argument. Unfortunately the Italian government has also seen fit to ban the noble custom of duelling, so we will have to get special permission. I might no longer be a young man, in fact my 60th birthday recently passed, but that is no matter. I will protect my honour or die!*

**Italo Santelli**, Coach of Hungarian Olympic fencing team

At the Paris Games, the fencers took their combat outside the Olympic stadium. Italo got government permission to hold the duel. He was to face the Italian captain on a barge off the coast of Italy. But Italo's son, Giorgio, thought that his father was too old for duelling. He insisted on fighting in his place. Giorgio Santelli won the duel in a mater of minutes, wounding the Italian captain on the side of the head.

# 1924 | PARIS, FRANCE
## *The Games of the VIII<sup>th</sup> Olympiad*

| | | | | | | | ❶ | ❷ | ❸ |
|---|---|---|---|---|---|---|---|---|---|
| 1924 | Paris | France | 44 | 17 | 2956 | 136 | USA | Finland | France |

Even though the previous Olympics had not been a financial success, there was keen competition to host the 1924 Games. At least nine countries said they wanted to be the host. Baron de Coubertin was desperate to have the Games return to Paris.

## The Baron's Last Games

This was to be the baron's last year as president of the IOC and he wanted his native country to make amends for the dreadful 1900 Games.

In the 28 years since he first thought of the Olympic Games, the Baron had seen them established as an international event. His dream of a male-only Games for honourable amateurs hadn't quite come true, but after some early hiccups, it was growing in size and popularity every four years.

## The Flying Finn

Finland did well in track and field again. The star of the Finnish team was Paavo Nurmi. He won gold medals in five events including the 5000-metre race and the 1500-metre race, even though he had less than an hour to rest between these two races. He won two more gold medals in team events and he also won the cross-country race.

Paavo was dedicated to running. His training was unusually intense and he carefully paced himself in every race using a stopwatch. He was rarely seen smiling. International journalists searched for a reason for Paavo's incredible speed. Rumours were spread that it was because his heart was twice normal size, because he ate only black bread and dried herring, or because he took cold baths. In the end the world decided he was just very fast.

## Cross-country Chaos

Long distance cross-country races had been run in the 1912 and the 1920 Olympics without getting a lot of attention. The 1924 cross-country race was such a disaster that it disappeared from the Olympic program forever.

On the day of the race it was over 40ºC (104ºF)—one of the hottest days ever known in Paris. The course chosen for the race was not a good one. The competitors were sometimes up to their knees in thistles. One by one runners collapsed from heat exhaustion, sunstroke or nausea caused by fumes from a nearby power generator.

Of the 39 runners who started the race, only 15 made it to the finishing line. The first one, apparently

*"There was something inhumanly stern and cruel about him, but Paavo Nurmi conquered the world by pure means: with a will that had supernatural powers."*

**Martti Jukola**, Finnish sports Journalist

unaffected by the heat and fumes, was Paavo Nurmi who hardly seemed to be tired at all. He was a full two minutes in front of the next runner.

## Bad Blood

France's rugby team were the European champions and were expected to easily beat the inexperienced American team. The Parisian people didn't take to the US rugby players. Newspapers printed stories about their bad behaviour off the field. The French were unimpressed when the Americans easily beat Romania, the only other team in the competition.

When it came to the final between France and America, there was nothing but bad feeling towards the US players. As the Americans ran onto the field, they saw that a wire fence had been put up around the field, separating the spectators from the players.

Every time an American player touched the ball, the crowd of 30 000 booed. At half time the French were still confident of a win, despite the fact that one of their star players had been carried off the field unconscious. The Americans beat the French 17–3. The crowd threw bottles. Fighting broke out between French and US supporters. Loud booing drowned out the American anthem and the US team needed a police escort to leave the field.

That was the last time rugby was played at an Olympic Games.

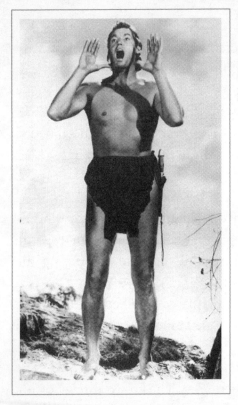

US Olympic swimmer Johnny Weissmuller as Tarzan. Weissmuller said, "The public forgives my acting because they know I was an athlete." (Sport the library)

## Jungle Johnny

The Parisian crowd hated the US rugby team, but they just loved one of the American swimmers. His name was Johnny Weissmuller. He won three gold medals for swimming and a bronze medal as a member of the water polo team. Not only did he impress the crowd with his amazing speed in the pool, during breaks he amused them with a comedy diving routine.

That wasn't the end of his fame though. When his sporting career came to an end, he became an actor. Because of his height (he was 6 foot 3 inches or 190 centimetres tall) and his athletic body he was chosen to play Tarzan in the movies. He starred in 12 Tarzan movies and another 14 as Jungle Jim.

## Olympic Ceremony

The Olympic motto *Citius, Altius, Fortius* was used for the first time at the 1924 Games. It is Latin for "faster, higher, stronger" and is meant to encourage Olympic athletes to strive for personal excellence. Baron de Coubertin introduced this new tradition.

There were three other American Olympic athletes who starred as Tarzan—there was also a Jane. Swimmer Eleanor Holm starred as Tarzan's girlfriend in *Tarzan's Revenge* in 1938.

Three flags were hoisted up flagpoles at the end of these Games—the flag of the host nation, the Olympic flag and the flag of the next Olympic host nation. This custom also became a permanent part of the Olympic Games. Ritual and ceremony were creating an Olympic tradition which added to the Games' importance.

# 1928 | AMSTERDAM, NETHERLANDS

### *The Games of the IX[th] Olympiad*

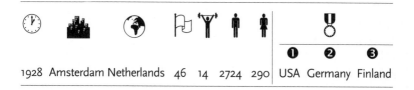

| 1928 | Amsterdam | Netherlands | 46 | 14 | 2724 | 290 | ❶ USA | ❷ Germany | ❸ Finland |
|------|-----------|-------------|----|----|------|-----|-------|-----------|-----------|

After more than 30 years as the person in charge of the Olympic Games, Baron de Coubertin had retired from his position as a president of the IOC. The committee honoured the Baron with the title of Perpetual President. This meant that he had an honorary position on the IOC for the rest of his life.

## The Courteous Games

The Baron must have felt very pleased with his efforts as he watched teams march into the stadium at the Opening Ceremony of the 1928 Games held in Amsterdam. Teams from 46 different nations were taking part—more than at any other Games. For the first time the teams didn't march in strict alphabetical order. At these Games, the Greek team marched first to recognise Greece's importance as the birthplace of the Olympic Games. Then came the rest of the teams in alphabetical order. Last came the team of the host nation, the Netherlands. This order has been used at every Games since.

For the first time, a flame was lit in a huge cauldron in the stadium. It burned throughout the Games just as it did in the Temple of Zeus at the ancient Games. The flame was to symbolise the spirit of the Games.

The Olympic venues were built on reclaimed land in Amsterdam. One end of the swimming pool later sank 15 centimetres (6 inches) giving the impression that the surface of the pool went uphill.

## Women *Can* Run

There was one thing that the Baron would not have been happy about— for the first time at an Olympics, women's track and field events were to be held.

Sportswomen had been trying to have athletics for women included at the Olympics since they began. So far women had only been allowed to compete in "ladylike" sports such as tennis and archery. By the 1920s, women's athletics clubs had started to form. Since they weren't allowed to take part in the Olympic Games, women athletes held their own international games. To the surprise of the all-male IOC, the women's games were a big success. Eventually, the IOC agreed to allow women to compete on a trial basis. They were only allowed five events—a 100-metre race, an 800-metre race, a 100-metre relay, discus throw and high jump—but it was a start.

> *"I am still against the participation of women in the Games. They have been included against my will."*
> **Baron de Coubertin**, IOC President 1896–1925

## Hockey Blitz

India made its Olympic debut at Amsterdam, competing in just one event—men's hockey. The team had only started playing at an international level two years earlier, but they blitzed their opponents and won the gold medal. Not a single goal was scored against them.

This began a winning streak for the Indian Olympic hockey team which lasted for 30 years. In 1928, India was a British colony, so although they competed separately they had to march behind the British flag and the British national anthem was played when they received their medals.

## The Falling Finn

Paavo Nurmi was back for his third Olympics. He won a gold medal in the 10 000-metre race and a silver medal in the

5000 metres. He also competed in an event he'd never tried before—the 3000-metre steeplechase. This event involves leaping over 28 hurdles and seven water jumps. During one of the heats, Paavo fell head first into a water jump. A French runner, Lucien Duquesne, stopped to help him out. After this courtesy, the Finnish champion didn't think it was polite to overtake the Frenchman so he ran alongside him for the rest of the race. He stopped at the finishing line and invited Lucien to cross the line first, but the Frenchman, knowing Paavo would have beat him, refused.

Paavo broke the stopwatch he always carried in the fall, but he went on to win a silver medal in this event.

## Ducks Crossing

This wasn't the only courteous act at the Amsterdam Olympics. The rowing events were held on a canal in Amsterdam. In a quarter final of the single sculls rowing event, Australian rower Henry Pearce was in the lead when he stopped in the middle of the race to let a mother duck and her ducklings swim in front of him. By that time another rower had overtaken him and was five lengths ahead. To the delight of spectators, Pearce caught up and went on to win a gold medal.

"We wore orange woollen shorts that we knitted ourselves...Old gents said how outrageous it was—a woman in shorts!"
**Mien Duchataeu**, Dutch Olympic runner

## Fainting Females

Lina Radke of Germany was one of the first female runners to win a gold medal in track and field events. She won the 800-metre race. It was an exciting race, with Japanese runner

Kinue Hitomi less than a second behind her. The race got a lot of publicity, but not because of the close finish. It was reported in the newspapers that several of the women collapsed from exhaustion after the race. Sensational headlines claimed that women athletes would grow old before their time if they ran such long races. It was widely believed that women couldn't cope with the strain and excitement of sport…and it was very unladylike.

Many male runners collapsed after races and one Olympic male runner had in fact died after a race, but no one ever suggested that male distance events be stopped. After the 1928 Games, however, women's races longer than 200 metres were banned until 1960.

# 1932 LOS ANGELES, USA
### *The Games of the X$^{th}$ Olympiad*

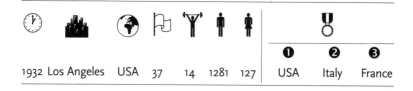

| | | | | | | | 1 | 2 | 3 |
|---|---|---|---|---|---|---|---|---|---|
| 1932 Los Angeles | USA | 37 | 14 | 1281 | 127 | | USA | Italy | France |

Los Angeles had been chosen as the host city for the 1932 Games way back in 1923. At that time, no one had any idea that when the 10$^{th}$ Games came around the world would be in the middle of an economic depression. For most teams, America was a long (and expensive) way from home. With

Cuba sent its Olympic team in a ship full of sugar and tobacco. These goods were sold at ports along the way to pay for the athletes' journey.

massive unemployment and people homeless and hungry, governments had more important things to worry about than sport. The Games were unpopular at home as well. The public thought the government should be spending money on feeding people rather than sporting events. There were protests with banners that read "Groceries not Games!".

The Games were due to start in July. By April not one nation had agreed to send a team and the two million tickets that had been printed remained unsold. It looked like the LA Games would be a disaster.

## Village of the Universe

The LA organising committee was not about to give up though. Fortunately a stadium had already been built. To encourage nations to send teams, they promised accommodation for the visiting teams in a "village of the universe". This consisted of 550 small houses specially built for the occasion in nearby hills. This was the first Olympic village.

The idea of an Olympic village for all athletes was a revolutionary one. National teams had previously preferred not to mix. Their coaches thought it was better if they didn't get too friendly with the opposition teams and kept their training secrets to themselves. It was cheaper for the organising committee though if the athletes were all in the same place. This way they were able to offer accommodation, food and travel to and from the stadium for a cost of just $2 per day for each athlete.

Another innovation at the 1932 Olympics was the first appearance of the Olympic Creed which has been displayed on the scoreboard at every Olympics since then.

## The Hollywood Games

Hollywood movie stars helped to promote the Olympic Games at home and overseas. Promises of cheap accommodation and reduced prices for travel changed the mood. Just weeks before the Games were due to open, nations started to announce that they would participate. The teams were smaller than in previous years, but 36 countries agreed to send teams to America. Tickets began to sell as well. Somehow, more than 100 000 people managed to find the money to attend the Opening Ceremony.

Stars such as Al Jolson, Charlie Chaplin and Marlene Dietrich volunteered to entertain visiting athletes, inviting them to their homes and entertaining them at nightclubs.

The three-tiered victory podium for gold, silver and bronze medallists was introduced at the LA Olympics. For the first time, there were medal ceremonies after each event, rather than at the end of each day.

> The most important thing in the Olympic Games is not to win but to take part, just as the most important thing in life is not the triumph but the struggle. The essential thing is not to have conquered but to have fought well.
>
> **Olympic Creed**

## Better Strokes

With perfect weather and first-class venues, the standard of the athletics was excellent. Many Olympic and world records were broken. The Americans were rewarded for their commitment to the Olympics by winning 103 medals—41 of them gold.

The Japanese swimming team had analysed underwater film of Johnny Weissmuller's swimming stroke—and improved on it. Thanks to their seven gold medals in the pool, Japan leapt up the medal count table to fifth place. One of the swimmers was 14-year-old Kusuo Kitamura who won the 1500-metre freestyle. He is still the youngest male Olympian ever to win an individual gold medal.

## Babe

The most popular athlete at the 1932 Olympics was, to the surprise of the IOC, a woman. Mildred Didrikson was an all-round athlete from Texas. The 21-year-old athlete was better known by her nickname "Babe".

She won two gold medals—one in the javelin throw, the other in the 80-metre hurdles. In the high jump, she tied with her team-mate Jean Shiley. They had a "re-jump". Again the two women jumped exactly the same height. The judges decided that Babe's jump was illegal, though, as she jumped head first instead of foot first. She had to be content with a silver medal.

Though Babe Didrikson qualified to compete in five events, Olympic

Babe Didrikson managed to get everyone who lived near her to trim their hedges to the same height so that she could use them to practise hurdling.

rules stated that female athletes could only compete in three, otherwise she may have won more medals.

## Minor Wrangles

There were only a few hiccups in an otherwise flawless Games. Paavo Nurmi arrived in LA, but was banned from competing because he had received money for running and was classified as a professional.

Swedish equestrian Bertil Sandström lost his second place in the dressage event because judges said he encouraged his horse with clicking sounds. He assured the judges that it was the saddle making the noise not him. They didn't believe him and he was demoted to last place.

The water polo also produced some drama when the Brazilian team lost to Germany. After the game, the Brazilian team attacked the referee because he had awarded 40 fouls against them. The Brazilians were disqualified from playing any more games.

## Dream Come True

The Los Angeles Olympics were a huge success. Around 1.25 million people went to see the events. The Games made $1 million profit. The concept of an Olympic village was a big hit. For the first time, athletes from all nations, from all walks of life, lived in the same comfortable conditions. They mixed together and formed friendships instead of ill will. The LA organising committee was nominated for a Nobel Peace Prize for this achievement. Baron de Coubertin's dream had come true. The Olympics had become a force for international harmony.

# 4 | FLICKERING FLAME

## Olympisch Stadion, Berlin, 4 August 1936

*I couldn't believe it when I first walked into the stadium. It
was packed, there must have been 100 000 people there.
Half the crowd was wearing uniforms—even the kids. It
looked more like a military event than the Olympics.
Thousands of flags and banners fluttered in the breeze.
Some were the flags of the nations competing, but most of
them were the red and black flag of the Nazi Party. When
Hitler appeared, everyone in the stadium suddenly stood up
and made the Nazi salute. It was creepy. It made the hairs
stand up on the back of my neck.*

*Black men aren't a common sight in Germany. It felt like
every second pair of eyes were on me. I can't read German,
so I haven't been able to read the papers, but one of the
American newspaper men told me what they were saying.*

*"If this Hitler guy thinks that black men are inferior," I
said to my coach. "I'm going to prove him wrong."*

*I'm competing in the long jump. It's just the qualifying
round. It should have been a breeze. I don't want to brag,*

but when I broke the long jump world record, it wasn't just by a quarter of an inch. I beat it by six inches.

My main rival is a German by the name of Luz Long. He's this lily-white guy with blue eyes and floppy blonde hair. He has to be one of Hitler's favourites.

I don't know why I got so nervous. I've done this a thousand times before. All I had to do was run about 150 feet along the runway and jump as far as I could into the pit. If I had a dollar for every time some wise guy's told me I'm too old to be playing in a sand pit, I'd be able to retire right now, a rich man.

Coach suggested I have a practice run-up, to loosen me up. I thought it was a good idea. I'd get a feel for the track.

I ran down the track, didn't jump, didn't even take off my track pants. Next thing I knew, the official was holding up a red flag. He counted it as my first jump! I told them it wasn't a real jump, I was just practising, but they ignored me. One of the judges noted the foul on his clipboard.

I was really riled. I peeled off my track suit. "I'll show 'em," I said to Coach.

I ran and jumped again. It was a good jump, or so I thought. I turned to the judge.

"Okay, Mr Stuck-up official," I said. "What did ya make of that?"

I couldn't believe it. He was waving the red flag again. Coach says I fouled. My foot touched the take-off board when I jumped. I only had one jump left to qualify.

Then Luz Long walked over to me, staring at me with

those blue eyes, pushing his blonde hair back off his face. I thought, "He's coming over to rub it in."

"If I was you," he said, "I'd take off further back. You only have to jump 7.15 metres."

I was sure he was taking the mickey out of me.

"You should be able to jump that far easily," he went on. "Something must be bothering you. Just calm down. You'll do very well."

Then I realised he was for real. He wanted to help. I thanked him and lay my towel down as a marker about six inches before the take-off line. I took some deep breaths. If I blew the next jump, I'd be out of the competition.

It wasn't the best jump I've ever done. The officials are measuring it now.

"Third jump, 7.18 metres."

That was close. If I'd jumped half an inch less, I wouldn't have qualified!"

Luz Long is coming back over to me. He's patting me on the shoulder.

"Don't worry. I'm sure you'll do better in the finals."

Now I know all 100 000 pairs of eyes are watching me. I can't see from here, but maybe Hitler himself is watching me.

**Jesse Owens**, US Olympic track and field athlete

Jesse Owens did do better in the long jump finals—much better. He won the gold medal, narrowly beating the courteous Luz Long. Luz was the first to go over and congratulate Jesse and the two athletes became firm friends.

# 1936 BERLIN, GERMANY
## The Games of the XI[th] Olympiad

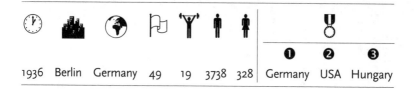

| | | | | | | | 1 | 2 | 3 |
|---|---|---|---|---|---|---|---|---|---|
| 1936 | Berlin | Germany | 49 | 19 | 3738 | 328 | Germany | USA | Hungary |

Berlin was awarded the next Olympic Games in 1928. Five years later, Adolf Hitler's Nazi Party came to power. Hitler realised that the Olympics were an opportunity to show the world the superiority of Germany under his rule. It also brought the Nazi Party's racist views to the IOC's attention.

Hitler's aim was to turn Germany into a country full of people superior to other people in the world. He called these people "Aryans". That meant that they were white and non-Jewish. World War II and the holocaust were still a few years in the future, but at the time of the games Jews were denied German citizenship as the Nazis tried to drive them out of Germany. This campaign affected athletes as well. Jewish sporting clubs were closed down and Jewish people were banned from joining German clubs. Jewish athletes were not allowed to compete in Olympic trials.

## The Hitler Games

At that time, Luz's helpful chat with Jesse was much more than a friendly gesture. At the 1936 Olympics, a German

Luz Long and Jesse Owens at the 1936 Berlin Games.
(Dr George Eisen)

talking to a black athlete was a bold political protest.

Hitler believed black people were inferior and was horrified when he realised that German athletes would have to compete against black athletes in the Olympics. He wanted black and Jewish people banned from taking part in his Olympics.

But racial discrimination is forbidden in the Olympic charter. If Germany was going to host the Games, no one could be banned because of their race, colour or religion. Hitler was told he had to allow Jewish people to try out for Olympic competition. In the end only one "half-Jew" who looked Aryan

In 1984 a street in Berlin was named after Jesse Owens.

joined the German Olympic team. This was Helene Mayer who was to compete in fencing.

Jewish people in America called for the US team to boycott the Games. The head of the US Olympic Committee was Avery Brundage (a future president of the IOC). Like Baron de Coubertin, he didn't want anything to stop the Olympics. He visited Germany himself. Though he would have seen anti-Jewish posters in the streets, he reported back that Jewish people weren't being treated any different to anyone else. No countries boycotted the Berlin Games.

> *"It took great courage for him to befriend me in front of Hitler. You can melt down all the medals and cups I have and they wouldn't be plating on the 24-carat friendship I felt for Luz Long at that moment."*
> **Jesse Owens**, US Olympic track and field athlete

## Spectacle

No expense was spared in making the Berlin Games the best Games ever. New facilities were built for every sport. As well as the main stadium there were nine other venues including a swimming pool, a hall for wrestling and weightlifting, and an open-air theatre for concerts. At the Opening Ceremony famous composer Richard Strauss conducted an Olympic hymn which he had composed himself. At night dozens of spotlights outlining the stadium pierced the night sky.

The Olympic village was well equipped with a library, theatre, hospital and swimming pool for the visiting athletes. It was set in pleasant surroundings with a lake and birch trees. There were also plenty of training facilities.

## Limited Success

The German Olympic team won more medals than any other country. They beat the Americans who had been at the top of the medal tally in eight out of 10 of the previous Olympics. German athletes dominated in gymnastics, rowing and equestrian events.

Other winners disproved Hitler's racist theories. A Japanese runner won the marathon. Japanese swimmers won four gold medals. Egyptian weightlifters won two gold medals. In the women's fencing, Helene Mayer, the only Jewish athlete in the German team, won a silver medal. The gold medal in this event was won by Hungarian Ilona Elek who was also Jewish. Eleven other medallists were Jewish or of Jewish descent.

The Americans were still victorious in track and field, and it was black American athletes who won most medals in these events. They won seven gold medals, three silver and three bronze—more athletics medals than any other country's entire team.

As well as medals, in 1936 Olympic winners were also given oak tree seedlings. Many athletes took their little trees home and planted them. A number are known to be still living.

## The Ebony Antelope

One of the black athletes was Jesse Owens, the star of the American track and field team. He was an exceptional athlete. At a sports championship the previous year, Jesse had broken five world records in 45 minutes. His long jump world record wouldn't be broken for another 25 years. At the Berlin Olympics he won four gold

Newspapers all over the world acknowledged the success of Jesse Owens and other black athletes.
(By permission of the United States Holocaust Memorial Museum)

medals. As well as the long jump, he won the 100-metre race, the 200-metre race and he was a member of the winning relay team.

Hitler and the Nazis weren't impressed by the success of the black athletes. It completely disproved their theory that blond-haired, white people were the superior race. The Nazi newspaper didn't report the black Americans' success, but the German public treated Jesse as the star of the Games. Crowds followed him wherever he went, clamouring for his autograph.

## Torch Relay

One innovation introduced at the Berlin Olympics has become a very important part of the Olympic ritual—the torch relay. Carl Diem had been associated with the German Olympic team since 1906 and was a good friend of Baron de Coubertin. It was his idea to light the Olympic flame at the site of the ancient games—Olympia. The flame was then carried all the way to Berlin. Three thousand runners took turns to carry the Olympic torch through seven countries.

The flame at Olympia was lit the same way it had been at the ancient Games—by the rays of the sun with priestesses in attendance. In ancient times the sun's rays shone on a shiny metal dish where they made some dry grass burst into flames. Nowadays a curved mirror is used to concentrate the sun's rays.

## Youngest Ever

Perhaps because of the excellent facilities, the standard of athletics at the Berlin Olympics was very high. Marjorie Gestring of the US was one of the successful athletes. She won a gold medal for springboard diving. She was only 13 years old. She is still the youngest person ever to win an individual Olympic gold medal.

## Hoodwinked

Though wary of Hitler's militaristic state, the world couldn't help but be impressed by the Berlin Olympics. The venues were the best ever seen and everything ran like clockwork. At the Berlin Olympics, Hitler presented his Nazi party as a peaceful, tolerant government. The German people were warm and friendly to their visitors. Newspapers around the world published articles praising the organisation of the Games and people wondered if perhaps the Nazis weren't as bad as everyone thought.

Two weeks after the Games, Hitler started preparing for war. The anti-Jewish signs went back up. The mask of international goodwill was dropped. By the time the next Olympics came around Hitler had declared war. It would be 12 years before the world saw another Olympic Games.

# 1948 | LONDON, ENGLAND
## *The Games of the XIV^{th} Olympiad*

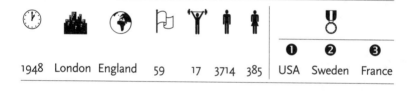

| 1948 | London | England | 59 | 17 | 3714 | 385 | USA | Sweden | France |
| --- | --- | --- | --- | --- | --- | --- | --- | --- | --- |
| | | | | | | | ❶ | ❷ | ❸ |

World War II lasted for six years and resulted in two Olympic Games being cancelled. It was 1948 before the next Games were held. And these Olympics were very different to the LA Games.

London was chosen as the host for this second post-war Games even though large parts of the city had been destroyed by bombs. There was still a shortage of houses for the residents of London, so the visiting athletes had to make do with army barracks and colleges. Though the war had ended three years earlier, food such as meat, eggs and butter was still in short supply.

A poster advertising the Games in London, 1948.
(Sport the library)

## Make-do Games

The British government had no money to spend on the Games. In fact, newspaper articles questioned whether the Games should be held at all. The British didn't try to match the spectacle of the 1936 Games. Instead they showed how the war had taught them to make do with what they had. No new venues were built. A temporary running track was laid in the Wembley Football Stadium for track and field events. Local pools were used for swimming and water polo.

## Olympic Losses

After such a long break, many of the athletes who had starred at the previous Olympics didn't reappear at the 1948 Games. Jesse Owens, despite his brilliance in 1936, never competed at another Olympics. Others, like Jesse's friend Luz Long, had been killed during the war.

Another person was missing from the Games. The person responsible for the very existence of the Olympics, Baron de Coubertin, had died in 1937 aged 74. In his will he requested that his body be buried in Lausanne, the home of the IOC headquarters in Switzerland. He wanted his heart to be buried in Olympia. His wish was granted and a marble memorial containing his heart now stands at Olympia.

## Old Hands

Some athletes were too old to compete now. Others managed to overcome disadvantages of age and succeed in 1948. Today, gymnastics is a sport in which competitors are thought to be old if they're in their 20s. Finnish gymnast Heikki Savolainen travelled to London for his fourth Olympic Games and won his first gold medal—at the age of 40. Ilona Elek won another gold medal for fencing even though she was now 41 years old.

## Growing Family

Germany was again not invited to London, nor was Japan. With so many countries still experiencing post-war economic difficulties, it seemed likely that there would be fewer national teams at the 1948 Olympics. There were in fact 10 more countries participating. The Olympic Games were becoming truly international as nations from all parts of the world, including Venezuela, Lebanon and Burma, joined the Olympic "family".

## Wrestling Turks

The Turkish wrestling team was victorious at the 1948 Games. They won six gold medals, four silver and a bronze. Turkey had only ever won one gold and one bronze medal at previous Olympics. When they returned to Turkey, the wrestlers were welcomed as heroes. The Turkish government rewarded them for their achievements and gave them presents including houses and large sums of money. Unfortunately, these rewards were considered as payments by the IOC. The successful wrestlers lost their amateur status and couldn't compete in the Olympics again.

## The Flying Dutchwoman

Dutch athlete Fanny Koen was an 18-year-old when she made her first Olympic appearance back in 1936, but she didn't make an impact. When she returned to Olympic competition in London she was 30 years old, her name was now Fanny Blankers-Koen. She was married with two children. She won four gold medals in the 100-metre race, the 200-metre race, the 80-metre hurdles and the 100-metre relay. She probably would have won more medals if Olympic rules hadn't limited her to four events.

People had barely got used to the idea of women running at all. Now they were astonished that a woman who had had two babies could break world records and win gold medals. She was criticised by some for not staying home with her children.

> "The people didn't like it, especially the women. They wrote to me that it was a shame that a mother of two children was running in little short shorts in a stadium."
>
> **Fanny Blankers-Koen**, Dutch Olympic runner

## In the Dark

The beginning of the 1948 Games had been held in unusually hot weather, but by the time the decathlon came around the weather had taken a turn for the worse. The 10 events of the decathlon take place over two days. On the first day athletes take part in the 100-metre dash, long jump, shot put, high jump and 400-metre run. On the second day of the 1948 decathlon it was raining. The athletes went out onto the track in the morning to compete in the 110-metre hurdles, discus throw, pole vault, javelin throw and 1500-metre run. Rain delayed the various events and the athletes were still out on the track at 10 o'clock in the evening.

Hungarian pistol shooter Károly Takács lost his right hand during the war when a grenade that he was holding exploded. He taught himself to shoot with his left hand and won a gold medal in 1948.

It was summer, but by the time 17-year-old American athlete Bob Mathias got out on the field for the javelin throw it was dark. There were no floodlights at Wembley Stadium, so officials arranged for cars to be driven onto the field so that Bob could see the take-off line by the light of their headlights.

The final event was the 1500-metre race. Bob, cold and exhausted, splashed through puddles as black mud splattered up his legs. He was barely able to see where he was going in the darkness. He made excellent time and won the event. It was only two months after he had graduated from high school. He is still the youngest person ever to win an Olympic gold medal in the decathlon.

## Games on TV

The post-war Olympics didn't produce any new

innovations for athletes. There were no stunning additions to the Olympic ceremonies. The only innovation on the sports field was pretty low-tech—the introduction of starting blocks for sprinters. Previously, runners had to dig holes to brace their foot when starting.

There had been one major technological advance in the 12 years since the last Olympics—television. Television programs were now being broadcast in England and people were able to watch the highlights of the Olympics on TV for the first time. Only about one in every 200 families had a TV, so not many people saw the broadcasts. It was, however, the introduction of the technology that would eventually bring the Olympic Games to more than half the population of the world.

# 1952 HELSINKI, FINLAND

## *The Games of the XV<sup>th</sup> Olympiad*

| | | | | | | | | ❶ | ❷ | ❸ |
|---|---|---|---|---|---|---|---|---|---|---|
| 1952 | Helsinki | Finland | 69 | 17 | 4407 | 518 | | USA | USSR | Hungary |

Helsinki, the capital city of Finland, is the smallest city ever to host an Olympic Games. In 1952 its population was less than 400 000. The city had to welcome more than 4000 athletes as well as officials and coaches. It was also expecting around 200 000 visitors to come and watch the Games, but all of the hotels in Helsinki together could only house 4000 people. The organising committee arranged accommodation for the visitors in schools, army barracks and private homes.

Horses in equestrian events must have an international passport to travel overseas just like people do.

## The Scandinavian Games

Helsinki was due to hold the 1940 Games before they were cancelled, and they had already built a stadium and a swimming pool. These were enlarged for the 1952 Games to cope with the growing interest in the Olympics.

The torch relay was now a permanent part of the Opening Ceremony and spectators and athletes alike were thrilled to see that the last torchbearer to run into the stadium was Paavo Nurmi. The legendary runner lit the Olympic flame.

## Politics

World War II was starting to fade from people's memories. Japan and Germany were invited to compete again. But other political issues troubled the IOC. Russian athletes took part in the Olympics for the first time in 40 years. But now Russia had swallowed a number of its neighbours and had grown into a major world power—the Union of Soviet Socialist Republics (USSR).

The USA has won the most medals in Olympic history—2116 altogether up to the year 2000. But if you compare the number of medals to population size, the USA comes in at number 26 (just ahead of Luxembourg). Finland is the winner with 296 medals, but a population of only five million people.

The USSR was a Communist country and it was keen to show that the Communist system was superior to the West. The Americans, as representatives of the largest capitalist country in the world, were just as determined to prove the opposite. Though the USSR and the USA did not go to war, there was a lot of tension between the two countries. There were threats of military attacks, there were economic sanctions and there was fierce competition in everything from space travel to sport. This period of history became known as the Cold War.

## Double Standard

Having the USSR team compete in the Olympics posed a problem for the IOC. It was known that the Communist government paid for their star athletes' training and rewarded them when they were successful. Other athletes in the past had been considered professional because of such payments and banned from competing in the Olympic Games. The Soviets denied that the government was supporting their athletes. Not wanting to ban the entire USSR team, the IOC turned a blind eye to the so-called "state amateurs". At the same time they continued to be very strict about amateurism in the teams from the West.

## Women on Horseback

No one questioned the involvement of female athletes in the Olympic Games anymore. The number of women at the 1952 Games reached 500 for the first time, but it was still a fraction of the number of men competing. Women were restricted to nine events, compared to 24 men's events. In 1952, women were allowed to compete in equestrian events for the first time. But there were no separate events for women. On horseback women competed against men.

Lis Hartel of Denmark became the first woman to win an Olympic equestrian medal. She won a silver medal in the individual dressage event. Lis's win was remarkable because her legs were paralysed below the knee and she needed help to get on and off her horse. Like Jim Thorpe, Lis was a victim of polio.

## Long Distance Champion

The star of this Olympics was undoubtedly Czechoslovakian long-distance runner Emil Zátopek. He entered the 5000-metre and 10 000-metre races. In the qualifying heats, he unnerved other competitors by chatting to them in several languages as he passed them. He won gold medals in both events.

Not satisfied with this success, he decided to run in the marathon as well, even though he'd never run a marathon before. He learned "on the job" by observing other more experienced runners during the race and even asking their advice along the way. When one runner sucked a lemon for refreshment and then slowed down, Emil decided this

> "I was unable to walk for a whole week after [the marathon], so much did the race take out of me. But it was the most pleasant exhaustion I have ever known."
>
> **Emil Zátopek**,
> Czechoslovakian
> Olympic runner

wasn't a good strategy. After all his competitors had either dropped out or fallen well behind, Emil chatted to spectators and policemen as he ran. He arrived in the stadium more than two and a half minutes in front of the next runner.

Emil's achievement of Olympic gold medals in the 5000-metre, 10 000-metre and marathon races has never been equalled.

## Cold War in Sport

Many Russians didn't like their Communist government, and the Soviet Olympic Committee was concerned that some of its athletes might try and escape to the West while they were in Helsinki. They insisted on having separate accommodation for their athletes, and the Finns had to build a second Olympic village to house them. To make sure there were no defections, the Soviets didn't bring any athletes who they thought were unhappy with the Communist system.

The battle for the most medals was narrowly won by the Americans. The Soviets didn't lose any of their athletes to the West, but an athlete from Romania, another Communist country, did defect. A sympathetic Finn whisked Romanian shooter Panait Calcai away in a car.

The Cold War would continue to effect the Games for many years to come.

# 5 FRIENDS AND FOES

## Olympic Pool, Melbourne, 28 November 1956

*I was honoured to be asked to referee an Olympic match and delighted to get to travel across the world to Australia. Who would have ever thought I would go to such a distant place at the bottom of the world? Water polo has never been the most popular Olympic sport, so I wasn't expecting my matches to attract much interest. I couldn't have been more mistaken. Usually it's the marathon or the 100-metre dash or a close swimming race that gets all the attention, but there was one particular water polo match that must have had more coverage in the newspapers than even those events.*

*Of course I'd heard the news from Europe about the USSR invading Hungary, so I knew this match between the USSR and Hungary would be tense, but I thought that the seriousness of an Olympic match would calm the emotions on both sides. I wasn't prepared for what happened.*

*The first two quarters weren't too bad, though the spectators' shouting got louder with each of the two goals*

71

that Hungary scored. There wasn't an empty seat in the place, and I'm sure that more than half of the 5000 spectators were Hungarians who had emigrated to Australia. It wasn't always encouragement they were shouting either. There were cries of "God save Hungary!" and "Freedom!" as well. (They were shouting in English, of course, so that the newspaper men would report it.) Every time a Soviet player got the ball, the spectators would boo and hiss. The other half of the crowd were cheering for the Hungarians too. If there were any there supporting the Soviets, they didn't dare admit it.

At half time the score was 2–0 in Hungary's favour. I thought the break would calm the players down, but that wasn't the case. Things only got worse.

I had barely blown my whistle to start the third quarter when the first fighting started. I sent a Soviet player to the exclusion box for elbowing a Hungarian. That was just the beginning. Every time I looked away, I could hear splashing and grunting behind me as players fought each other. I couldn't stop it. I had to keep my attention on the ball. I would have needed eyes in the back of my head to control that game.

Even the players in my view were at it. There was kicking, punching, eye gouging. It was like a wrestling match only with 14 fighters in the ring all at once. Though the Soviets seemed to start the conflict, the Hungarians were quick to join in…and with even more hostility. I saw one Soviet player disappear beneath the water and I thought for a moment he wasn't going to come up again. He did, but he was groggy and struggling to keep himself conscious.

The crowd only made matters worse. They were roaring support for the Hungarians. Then the roar of jubilance turned to a scream of rage. I turned to find the Soviet left half, Prokopov, punching Hungarian centre forward, Zádor, in the face. Zádor came up spluttering. Blood from a cut above his eye was staining the water red. I called time-out and sent Prokopov out of the pool. When the match restarted, the water was churning like a whirlpool with all the kicking and punching underwater.

The organisers had obviously been expecting trouble and had put up a wire fence between the spectators and the pool. The crowd was furious by this time. Many spectators jumped the fence and were shouting abuse at the Soviet team and even spitting at them. Thankfully the second hand on the clock finally crawled around to the finishing time.

I don't think anyone heard the timekeeper's whistle.

"Will all persons not directly connected with the water polo kindly leave the concourse," an announcer repeated again and again, but if anyone heard, they took no notice. The Soviets were too afraid to come out of the water. The crowd was ready to attack them. Fortunately, four policemen arrived to control the scene.

"The winner is Hungary, 4–0," the announcer shouted.

That changed the tune of the crowd's shouts from anger to delight. I left the poolside, shaking like a leaf.

**Mr S Zuckerman**, Swedish water polo referee

This was the worst display of violence between competitors in Olympic history. And an example of how the aggression of war can cause aggression in sport. But unlike rugby, which was taken from the list of Olympic sports after a particularly brutal game, water polo is still an Olympic sport today.

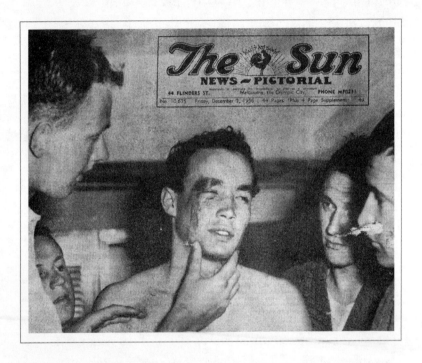

Hungarian star Ervin Zádor after rough water-polo match.
(Courtesy of The Herald & Weekly Times Ltd., Newspaper Collection, State Library of Victoria)

# 1956 | MELBOURNE, AUSTRALIA

*The Games of the XVI^th Olympiad*

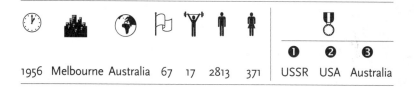

| | 1956 | Melbourne | Australia | 67 | 17 | 2813 | 371 | USSR | USA | Australia |
|---|---|---|---|---|---|---|---|---|---|---|

There was a great deal of political unrest in the world at the time of the 1956 Olympics. America and the USSR were engaged in Cold War politics. Conflict had broken out between Israel and Egypt over the Suez Canal. Britain and France became involved. Worse still, only three weeks before the Games the USSR invaded Hungary. Spain, the Netherlands and Switzerland withdrew from the Games in protest of this Soviet aggression.

The dream of a record number of competing nations looked like turning into a nightmare of a record number of nations refusing to attend. In the end 11 nations changed their mind and decided not to compete.

## The Down-under Games

When a group of people first sat down to discuss the idea of holding the Olympic Games in Melbourne, they didn't really think it would be possible. For a start they only had

When US weightlifter Charles Vinci weighed in before his Olympic event, he discovered he was 200 g (seven ounces) overweight. He managed to lose the weight in the 15 minutes before the event started—by having a haircut! He won the gold medal.

funds of six pounds seven shillings and ten pence. Secondly, Melbourne was a long way from the rest of the world. But when the IOC voted to decide who would host the 1956 Games, Melbourne won by one vote.

The IOC was very nervous about having the Olympics so far from Europe. The Games had never been held in the Southern Hemisphere before. There was the problem of the seasons. The Games were usually held between July and August—in Australia that was winter. The year before the Games, IOC President Avery Brundage, was so worried that he flew to Australia to check on the progress. He wasn't impressed by what he saw. Workers building the Olympic Village and renovating the Melbourne Cricket Ground were all on strike. It seemed impossible that the venues would be ready on time. Mr Brundage threatened to hold the Games in Philadelphia instead.

## Quarantine

Another headache for the IOC was Australia's strict quarantine laws for live animals. Horses from other countries could only enter Australia after they had spent six months in isolation, to make sure they didn't have any diseases. This made it impossible to have the equestrian events in Melbourne. Instead, they were held in Sweden earlier in the year.

## Ready to Go

The IOC needn't have worried. Melbourne was ready for the Games on time. The Games were held in November—late spring. Teams didn't have to make four-week ship voyages to get to the Games. Pressurised aircraft had been built and for the first time, commercial airlines were flying passengers to Australia. The trip from Europe took a mere 30 hours!

The Melbourne Cricket Ground was finished. So was the Olympic Village. The Melbourne organisers refused to provide separate accommodation for the Russian athletes and they stayed in the Olympic Village with the rest of the athletes. For the first time, male and female athletes shared the same village...though they were separated by a three-metre (10 foot) barbed wire fence.

## Travelling Companions

Some were surprised that Hungary still attended the Games. In fact when the USSR invaded Hungary, 17 members of the Hungarian Olympic team were already on their way to Melbourne—aboard a Russian merchant ship. Their companions onboard were 91 members of the USSR Olympic team.

*"I've never been in a game like this. It wasn't a water polo match, it was pure boxing under water."*
**Ervin Zádor**, Hungarian Olympic water polo player

## Aussie Swimmers

Looking back, it seems like the Melbourne Games was all about politics, but to most spectators it was all about sport. Australians flocked to see the Games. They were rewarded by seeing their athletes win more medals than at any previous Olympics.

Most successful was the Australian swimming team. Australian swimmers won 20 out of a possible 36 medals in the pool. This included all eight gold medals in the freestyle swimming events.

Dawn Fraser had started swimming at the age of five to improve her asthma. Her swimming talent had been recognised by the time she was 13. She celebrated her first Olympic appearance by winning two gold and one silver medal.

Seventeen-year-old Murray Rose made headlines by becoming the youngest Olympic triple gold medallist. He won gold medals in the 400-metre and 1500-metre swimming events and was also a member of the winning relay team. He also attracted media attention because he was a vegetarian, which was unusual in 1956.

"War, politics and nationality will be all forgotten, what more could anybody want, if the whole world could be made as one nation...THEY MUST NOT MARCH but walk freely and wave to the public...It will show the whole world how friendly Australia is."

**John Ian Wing**, Melbourne apprentice carpenter

Another Australian swimmer, Jon Henricks, made swimming history. He was the first Olympic athlete to shave his head and body to improve speed in the water. He also won two gold medals.

## Closing Harmony

The Hungarians were proud they had won nine medals for their country, but 45 members of the Hungarian Olympic team didn't return home.

Murray Rose is congratulated by Tsuyoshi Yamanaka. (Courtesy of The Herald & Weekly Times Ltd., La Trobe Collection, State Library of Victoria)

Instead they asked for political asylum and stayed in Australia or went to live in Europe.

A few days before the end of the Games, a young Chinese-born Australian by the name of John Ian Wing wrote to the Melbourne organising committee. He suggested that instead of marching in straight lines behind their country's flag, as they did in the Opening Ceremony, athletes should walk together informally at the Closing Ceremony.

It wasn't until the last day of the Olympics that John's idea was okayed. The athletes responded to it immediately, mixing together, linking arms and waving to the crowd. Since then the Closing Ceremony has always been the same. One young person's idea became a permanent part of Olympic tradition. Just as John had hoped, people forget about war and politics and, just for a moment, the world is like one nation.

# 1960 | ROME, ITALY
### *The Games of the XVII<sup>th</sup> Olympiad*

| ⏱ | 🏙 | 🌍 | 🚩 | 🏋 | 🚹 | 🚺 | | 🥇 ① | 🥈 ② | 🥉 ③ |
|---|---|---|---|---|---|---|---|---|---|---|
| 1960 | Rome | Italy | 83 | 17 | 4738 | 610 | | USSR | USA | Italy |

In 1960 the Cold War between the USA and the USSR was at its height. Germany was split in two. The People's Republic of China and Taiwan were arguing over which was the real China. Yet the Rome Games were surprisingly non-political.

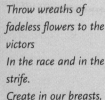

*Throw wreaths of fadeless flowers to the victors*
*In the race and in the strife.*
*Create in our breasts, hearts of steel!*
**Words from the Olympic Anthem**

## The Scenic Games

The organisers thought Rome was the perfect place to hold the Olympic Games. A modern city with ruins of ancient buildings scattered about it, Rome seemed to link the ancient and the modern Games. The events were held in a mixture of new stadiums and ancient monuments more than a thousand years old. The gymnastics took place among the ruins of the Baths of Caracalla, the public baths where ancient Romans had bathed. The wrestling was held in the Basilica of Constantine, a large building used as a court and a marketplace which was built in 312 CE. Ironically it was the Roman Emperor Theodosius who banned the ancient Olympics, but no one was mentioning that in 1960.

Once the Games began, politics took a back seat. The women's 800-metre race was reintroduced after a break of 32 years—and all the competitors survived. The USSR continued its total domination in gymnastics by winning 11 gold medals.

Spectators watched as Peter Snell from New Zealand came from nowhere to beat the world favourites in the 800-metre race, winning the first gold medal for New Zealand since 1936. Peter still holds the 800-metre record for a New Zealander.

## Barefoot Victory

Perhaps the highlight of the Games was the marathon. There were many "firsts" at this marathon. This was the first Olympic marathon that didn't start or finish in the main stadium. It was also the first time there had been a false start and the race had to be restarted. For the first time in Olympic history the race was run at night. The route was lit by blazing torches which added to the drama of the event.

Because of the hot weather, British athlete Don Thompson prepared for the walking race by working out in a bathroom full of heaters and boiling kettles.

Moroccan runner Rhadi Ben Abdesselem was the favourite to win the race, but as he pulled ahead of the pack, there was another runner at his side. It was Abebe Bikila, an imperial guard in his homeland, Ethiopia. No one had heard much about this man. Spectators were intrigued because he ran barefoot. The two runners ran side by side for most of the race. Abebe made his final move as he ran past the Obelisk of Axum. This is an ancient monument which the Italians had plundered from Ethiopia 25 years earlier. Perhaps this was what inspired this victory for his country on Italian soil. Abebe surged ahead of his rival and won the marathon in world record time. Here was another "first". Abebe was the first black African to win an Olympic gold medal.

## The Greatest

Meanwhile an African-American was making his mark in the boxing ring. He was an 18-year-old by the name of Cassius Clay. He won a gold medal in the light-heavyweight division.

When he returned home to the USA, Cassius was given a hero's welcome. He was so proud of his medal that he wore it all the time. He wore it so much that he discovered the medal wasn't solid gold. The gold plating wore away to reveal lead underneath.

But his international fame didn't make any difference to his civil rights at home. He was barred from eating in whites-only restaurants. On one occasion he showed the waitress his medal but it didn't make any difference. A white biker gang chased him away and beat him up. After

Olympic gold medallist Cassius Clay changed his name to Muhammad Ali and became the most famous boxer of all time.
(Sport the library/Neil Leifer)

that he took his medal and threw it in a river. Later he converted to Islam and changed his name to Muhammad Ali. He went on to win the world heavyweight championship three times and become the most famous boxer ever.

## Olympics on the Box

There was live television coverage of the Olympics for the first time in Rome. People in 18 European countries watched the Olympics live on television.

The television audience suddenly leapt from a few thousand to millions. TV networks from around the world were clamouring to be allowed to broadcast the Olympics. An American network paid almost $400 000 for TV rights. This seemed like a staggering amount in 1960, but it is a fraction of the amount paid by TV networks today.

## Death on the Track

There was one low point of the Rome Olympics and it was a tragic one. During the 100-kilometre team cycling race, Danish cyclist Knut Jensen suddenly fell off his bike and fractured his skull. He was rushed to hospital, but died soon after. At first it was thought that he had been affected by sunstroke and his head injuries were the cause of death. It was later discovered that he had in fact died of a drug overdose. He had taken drugs to improve his performance. This didn't cause a big fuss. Though sporting officials around the world were becoming concerned about drug use, there were still no Olympic rules that banned it.

# 1964 | TOKYO, JAPAN
*The Games of the XVIII<sup>th</sup> Olympiad*

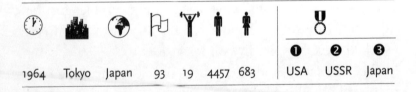

| 🕐 | 🏙 | 🌍 | 🏳 | 🏋 | 🧍 | 🧍‍♀️ | 🏅 | | |
|---|---|---|---|---|---|---|---|---|---|
| | | | | | | | ❶ | ❷ | ❸ |
| 1964 | Tokyo | Japan | 93 | 19 | 4457 | 683 | USA | USSR | Japan |

The Games had already been held on three different continents in the world—now it was Asia's turn to host the Olympic Games. The Japanese spared no expense on their preparations for the Olympics. They spent millions of dollars on improving highways and public transport, including two new lines on the underground railway.

# The Space-age Games

Since the last Olympics, the world had entered the space age—men had travelled in space, and satellites beamed TV pictures all over the world. For the 1964 Olympics, Tokyo was transformed into a space-age city with swirling raised freeways and stunning sporting venues. The National Gymnasium and its smaller baseball annexe, with their sweeping curves and spires looked like buildings from a futuristic movie.

During the semi-finals of the 1000-metre cycling sprint, the two competitors balanced on their cycles without moving for 21 minutes and 57 seconds each waiting for the other to lead off. This tactic is no longer allowed.

The athletes had changed their image as well. Gone were the dark, formal uniforms. Some of the female athletes were wearing fashionable outfits—the British wore pink suits, the Australians yellow dresses, the Polish women wore mauve. The men too were dressed in brighter colours—the Mexicans in red blazers, the Italians in bright blue. Athletes from African nations proudly wore their traditional robes, the Americans wore cowboy hats, Turkish athletes wore fezzes.

In previous Games, the last runner of the Olympic torch relay had always been a famous sports person. At the Tokyo Games, the person who entered the stadium and lit the Olympic flame was not an athlete. He was a young man called Yoshinori Sakai who had been born near Hiroshima on the day that the atomic bomb was dropped on that city.

"The formal opening ceremony was beautiful indeed, but tonight all barriers of nationality and race have dropped away...This moment brings tears to my eyes and warms my heart as if understanding for the first time what world peace would be like."
**Japanese commentator** at the Closing Ceremony, 1964

## Most Medals

The host nation was most successful in gymnastics and wrestling, winning five gold medals in each. The star of the gymnasium, however, was Russian Larisa Latynina. This was Larisa's third Olympic Games. At 30, she was old by gymnastic standards but she won two gold medals, a silver and two bronze. This brought her total number of Olympic medals to 18, including nine gold. This is still the record for the most Olympic medals won by any athlete.

## Dutch Surprise

Japan had managed to get judo included as an Olympic sport. This was one sport that the host nation was confident it would do well in. This form of martial arts had been practised in Japan for centuries, but it was a new sport in the West. There were four judo events at the 1964 Games. Japan won three gold medals, but was defeated in the open event. Dutch judo expert Antonius Geesink won this event. Japanese judo followers were so shocked they wept in the streets. The Japanese champion, Akio Kaminaga, had to be content with a silver medal and an unusual record. In one of the preliminary rounds he "threw" his opponent in six seconds. It was the shortest Olympic contest ever.

## Souvenir

The Americans dominated in the swimming pool, winning 14 gold medals in 18 events. One of the other gold medallists was Australia's Dawn Fraser. She won the 100-metre freestyle for the third time in a row, bringing her career medal tally to four gold and four silver.

Dawn had always enjoyed playing jokes. She was always getting into trouble for something, whether it was wearing the wrong colour tracksuit or going to parties and staying out late. She got into a lot of trouble at the Tokyo Games. Australian officials had banned those athletes who were competing in the first days of the Games from attending the Opening Ceremony. Dawn defied the ban and marched with the other athletes. Then she was caught trying to steal a Japanese flag from outside the Imperial Palace as a souvenir. She was arrested. She apologised and the police released her and presented the flag to her as a gift. The Australian Olympic Committee wasn't as forgiving. They banned her from competition for 10 years and Dawn never swam in another Olympic Games.

## Banned

The IOC could no longer ignore South Africa's racist apartheid system which discriminated against the black population. Apartheid was a government policy introduced in 1948 which set out different rights for black and white people. Black people couldn't vote. They could only live in certain

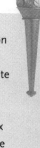

Abebe Bikila won his second marathon despite having his appendix removed just six weeks before the race.

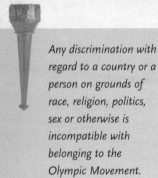

*Any discrimination with regard to a country or a person on grounds of race, religion, politics, sex or otherwise is incompatible with belonging to the Olympic Movement.*

**Olympic Charter,** Section 3.2

areas and get particular low-skill jobs. Black children had to go to different schools to white children. There were separate black and white areas in all public places from beaches to buses.

Many people in the world opposed these racist laws. Countries refused to trade with South Africa or play sport with them. South Africa was banned from taking part in the Tokyo Games and didn't compete again until 1992 after apartheid ended.

## Big

There was still a record number of countries taking part in the Games. In the early years of the Olympic Games, organisers had been worried about how few countries were involved. Now it was concerned that the Olympic Games were getting too big. As the Olympics grew, so did the cost of staging the Olympics. Over the next years, the huge cost would become a serious problem for host nations.

# 6 | BLOOD, SWEAT AND TEARS

## Estadio Olímpico, Mexico, 12 October 1968

*I don't have to run very far, less than a kilometre. I don't have to run very fast, in fact I'm just jogging. I have no competitors. I'm the only one running. But this is the most important race of my life. The torch is spluttering in my hand. The flame is strong. I'm not sure how it works. I lit it from the last torchbearer's torch. It's a simple design. A black handle that sits comfortably in my hand and a fluted cylinder made of a silvery metal. At the top, each flute becomes a letter. Together they spell out Mexico 68.*

*My torch is just one of 3000 used in the Olympic torch relay. Each one has been carried by a different runner. Together we have brought the Olympic Flame all the way from Olympia in Greece, here to Mexico City. That's a long way. More than 13 000 kilometres.*

*The flame crossed oceans as well, following the same route as Christopher Columbus when he came on his voyage of discovery. From Olympia, runners carried it to the port of Piraeus. Then the flame went by ship to Genoa in Italy, the* town where Columbus was born. An Italian ship took it to Barcelona the port in Spain from where the explorer embarked. A Spanish ship carried the flame to the island of San Salvador, the first place in the New World that Columbus landed. From there a Mexican ship brought it to Veracruz and 17 swimmers carried the flame ashore. Finally it was on Mexican soil. Then runners relayed it here to Mexico City. To me.

The organisers explained its importance to me. A flame burned throughout the Games in ancient times and a flame will burn throughout these Games here in Mexico. The flame is a symbol of the purity of the Games. I think it also symbolises peace. I hope the Games will be peaceful. I hope the world remembers the 1968 Games as a wonderful celebration of sport and harmony.

The Games haven't begun yet. They can't begin until I finish my task. I am in the tunnel now. It is cool and dark. I'm running towards the light at the end of the tunnel. My heart is beating as fast as if I had run all the way from Olympia myself. It's not beating from exhaustion. It's fear. What if I drop the torch? What if I'm remembered as the only athlete in history to allow the Olympic flame to go out?

The name of the last person to carry the Olympic torch is always kept a secret. It's usually someone important like the host country's most famous athlete. They've made a change this time. I am an athlete, a hurdler. I'm not famous though. I've won a few championships in Mexico, but when I run out into the light, few people will know who I am.

*Certainly the people watching on televisions in other countries won't know my name. They'll all be surprised to see me though.*

*The stadium is quiet, hushed. A shout goes up as I emerge into the stadium. The light is blinding after the tunnel. Just as I expected, the shout has a ring of surprise, but pleasure too, I think.*

*Now the cheers of the crowd have grown to a roar as I run around the track. My eyes are used to the light now. I have never seen so many people all in one place. My legs are shaking. Not far to go. I can see my goal ahead. My arm is aching but I'm still holding the torch high. It hasn't let me down. It is burning as bright as ever. I've reached the flight of steps. They are covered with bright pink carpet. I have to climb them. There are 92 steps, I know. I don't stumble, not once. I've reached the top. There is a huge cauldron on a platform. I lower my torch, dip it into the cauldron. It bursts into flame. The cheering of the crowd is deafening.*

*They might not know my name but they will remember me.*

**Enriqueta Basilio**, Mexican Olympic hurdler and torchbearer

Enriqueta Basilio was the first woman to light the Olympic flame. She competed in the hurdles race at the 1968 Games but didn't win a medal.

# 1968 MEXICO CITY, MEXICO

## The Games of the XIX<sup>th</sup> Olympiad

| | | | | | | | 1 | 2 | 3 |
|---|---|---|---|---|---|---|---|---|---|
| 1968 | Mexico City | Mexico | 112 | 20 | 4750 | 780 | USA | USSR | Japan |

Many people were concerned about the choice of Mexico City as the next Olympic host. Mexico is not a wealthy country and many people thought that it wasn't right for a poorer country to be spending millions of dollars on a sports event. The Mexican government thought it was a good investment. They believed that it would boost Mexico's image in the world and help its tourist industry.

Ten days before the Games there was a violent anti-government student demonstration. The Mexican government didn't want anything to jeopardise the Games. The army was called in. They opened fire and killed 250 students.

The Games went ahead. It seemed nothing would make the IOC stop the Olympic Games.

## The Elevated Games

Mexico City is 2240 metres (7350 feet) above sea level. The

higher you climb, the lower the air pressure. There isn't less oxygen at higher altitude, but the lower air pressure means you actually breathe in less oxygen. Therefore there is less oxygen travelling in the bloodstream to muscles. This has a big effect on athletes. It means an athlete has to breathe faster to get enough oxygen, so the heart beats faster and the athlete becomes exhausted quicker.

Doctors were concerned that athletes who weren't used to high altitudes could damage their hearts or lungs. They thought some might even die. Athletes and officials were concerned that the high altitude would also affect the results.

Building at the Olympic village site in Mexico was delayed while archeologists excavated an Aztec pyramid over 1000 years old which workers had unearthed.

## Breathless

The very first race proved that concerns were well founded. During the 10 000-metre race, two runners collapsed and were carried off on stretchers. When Australian runner Ron Clarke reached the finish line, he was staggering and uncoordinated. He collapsed and was unconscious for 10 minutes. He came sixth. His time was more than a minute slower than his previous Olympic time. The runners who took the five places ahead of Ron were all from countries with higher altitudes whose bodies were used to the conditions.

The predictions were right. No world records were beaten in longer events at the Mexico Olympics. Many competitors collapsed from exhaustion and doctors had to give oxygen to 16 athletes.

## Giant Leap for Bob

The story wasn't the same for short events though. In events less than 2.5 minutes, 24 world records and 56 Olympic records were beaten. Some of the records weren't just broken, they were smashed to pieces.

Usually previous records are broken by fractions of seconds or, in the case of the jumps, millimetres. In the long jump, American Bob Beamon beat the world record by more than half a metre (21 inches). The jump was so long that the special optical measuring equipment didn't reach that far. The officials had to find a tape measure. The result was put on the scoreboard in metres. Bob wasn't used to the metric system so he still wasn't sure how far he'd jumped. When someone converted the result to feet and inches, Bob was so stunned he collapsed to his knees in a seizure. The other contestants were totally demoralised by this amazing jump and no one came close to Bob's leap. His record wasn't beaten for 25 years.

Two horses died during the equestrian events in 1968. One fell in a rain-swollen stream and was swept away. The other broke its leg and had to be shot. Horses also died at the 1936 and 1960 Olympics.

## Short and Sharp

The reason for the success of the athletes in short events is that the low air pressure offers less resistance, so they can jump higher and further. In short running events, the negative effects of high altitude don't have time to take effect.

Technology also helped athletes at the 1968 Olympics. Fibreglass poles were used in the pole vault. Dick

Fosbury introduced a new style of head-first jump in the high jump. This was made less dangerous by the introduction of foam pads to land on instead of sand or sawdust. On the running track there were no more cinders, but a new synthetic track with a tufted surface like a mat. It provided an even running surface, with good traction and it never got muddy or soggy with rain.

## Last

John Akhwari, from the African country of Tanzania, didn't do very well in the marathon. In fact, he came last. He fell during the race and badly injured his leg. Spectators thought that he would pull out of the race, but he struggled on even though he was in a great deal of pain. He eventually limped over the finish line with his leg wrapped in a bloody bandage an hour after the winner. Though many spectators had left the stadium by this time, those who remained cheered the courageous runner as if he was the winner.

> "My country didn't send me 7000 miles to start a race, they sent me 7000 miles to finish it."
> **John Akhwari**, Tanzanian Olympic marathon runner

## Small Victory

Once again, just months before the Olympic Games, the USSR invaded a country. This time it was Czechoslovakia. Once again, the IOC didn't ban the USSR from the Games for this aggression. When the Czechoslovakian team marched onto the stadium during the Opening Ceremony, the crowd cheered them loudly.

Worldwide, the favourite athlete at the Mexican Games was Czech gymnast Vera Cáslavská. After her country was invaded, Vera was afraid that she would be arrested by the Soviets because she had publicly protested against the USSR. She didn't want to be in jail during the Olympics, so she hid in the mountains. She had to do her final training in a field.

To the delight of the spectators at the Olympics, Vera won four gold medals, beating Soviet gymnasts. The Mexican crowd applauded loudest for her floor exercise routine which she performed to the tune of the "Mexican Hat Dance".

## Black Power

Politics also found their way onto the athletics track. The US track and field team again consisted of many African-American athletes. After the 200-metre race, the gold medal winner, Tommie Smith, and the bronze medallist, John Carlos, decided to protest about continuing discrimination against black people in America. They walked up to collect their medals wearing black socks and no shoes to symbolise black oppression. When they climbed onto the winners podium and the US anthem started to play, they bowed their heads and both raised a black-gloved hand clenched into a fist. This was the salute of the Black Power Movement which was trying to improve the civil rights of black Americans. Silver medallist, Peter Norman from Australia, wore a civil rights badge to show he supported the protest.

The IOC insisted that Smith and Carlos be sent home.

Tommie Smith and John Carlos protest about discrimination against black people in America. (Sport the library)

## Testing, Testing

The IOC was slow to respond to growing drug abuse at the Olympics, but finally they took action. They made a list of substances that athletes were not allowed to use. Random drug tests were performed on Olympic athletes for the first time in Mexico. Only one athlete, a Swedish pentathlon competitor, was found positive. The banned substance he had used was alcohol.

There were other new tests on athletes at the 1968 Olympics, but they were performed only on the female athletes. The IOC was concerned that men might be posing as women in order to win medals, so they checked that the female athletes were, in fact, female.

In 1966 and 1967, sex tests were performed at international sporting competitions. Female athletes had to parade naked in front of a panel of doctors. Understandably, the athletes complained about this embarrassing experience.

The IOC decided to use a chromosome test using a smear of saliva from inside the cheek. In 28 years of testing no males were found pretending to be females. Instead many women were found to have natural genetic abnormalities. They were often banned from participating, even though these conditions gave them no advantage over other athletes. Sex tests were discontinued after the 1996 Olympics.

Testing for performance-enhancing drugs seems to be a permanent part of the Games. The people making the drugs are always a step ahead of those who are developing tests to detect them.

# 1972 | MUNICH, WEST GERMANY

*The Games of the XX<sup>th</sup> Olympiad*

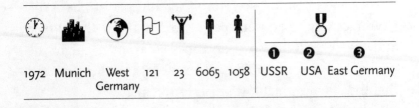

| | 1972 | Munich | West Germany | 121 | 23 | 6065 | 1058 | ❶ USSR | ❷ USA | ❸ East Germany |
|---|------|--------|--------------|-----|----|------|------|--------|-------|----------------|

A German city was the host of the Olympic Games for the second time in 1972. The organisers of the Munich Olympics wanted to erase the memory of the 1936 Games. They wanted to show the world that the modern Germany was a democratic, friendly, free and easy place, nothing like it was under the racist Nazi regime that had held the Games in 1936. Unfortunately, the 1972 Games are remembered for a different reason.

## Rebuilding

The main stadium was built on a site covered in rubble from World War II. It seemed to symbolise Germany's desire to bury its aggressive history. Many millions of dollars were spent making the venues the best ever. A graphic artist designed a modern decorative theme that would link all of the Games venues and the city itself. The first Olympic mascot came in the shape of Waldi, a soft toy Dachshund dog with blue, green and orange stripes who proved to be very popular.

For 10 days, spectators had been following the exciting events of the Games with keen interest. Then suddenly the eyes of the world turned from the track and the pool to the Olympic Village.

## The Terror Games

The German public awoke on 6 September to shocking news. A group of Palestinian terrorists had broken into the Olympic Village and taken 11 members of the Israeli Olympic team hostage. The terrorists, calling themselves the Black September Movement, were demanding the release of 200 political prisons in Israel. Two Israelis—a wrestling coach and a weightlifter—had already been killed. The terrorists threatened to kill the hostages, one every hour, if their demands were not met.

The Israeli government refused to negotiate with the terrorists. The situation was in the hands of the Germans. The German government had no previous experience with terrorism and was completely unprepared for such a terrible incident.

## Black September

The Games were suspended as the horrifying events unfolded. The German authorities tried to rescue the hostages, but a German television crew broadcast the rescue attempt and the terrorists watched their every move on TV. Eventually the German authorities pretended to agree to the terrorists' demands and transported them to an airport. Inexperience and poor communications resulted in a disastrous attempt to kill the terrorists as they transferred to helicopters. Only five marksmen were positioned to shoot the terrorists. In the gun battle that followed, all the Israeli hostages were killed. Five Palestinians, a policeman and a helicopter pilot also died.

## Grief

The Olympic Stadium filled with people again on 7 September, but this time it was for a memorial service. As the stunned world looked on, the Games organisers had to decide whether the Games would continue. Many people thought that it was disrespectful to continue after such a terrible event. The IOC decided that the Games

The three surviving terrorists never went to trial. They were handed over to other Palestinian terrorists after a plane hijack the following month.

would continue. The remaining Israeli athletes went home. Three other countries sent their teams home as a mark of respect. In a subdued atmosphere, planned events for the last days resumed.

## The Games Continue

The sporting achievements at the 1972 Games were overshadowed by the murder of the Israeli team members. Many athletes had already made their mark on the records before the terrorist attack.

*"We cannot allow a handful of terrorists to destroy the nucleus of international goodwill we had in the Olympic Movement—The Games must go on."*
**Avery Brundage**, IOC President 1952–1972

American swimmer Mark Spitz competed in seven events in eight days. He won gold medals and beat world records in every race, and became the only athlete ever to win seven gold medals at one Olympic Games. In the women's swimming events 15-year-old Australian Shane Gould won three gold medals, a silver and a bronze. Another Finnish champion, Lasse Viren, emerged to win two gold medals on the track. In the 10 000-metre race, he was in fifth place when he tripped and fell about halfway through the race. He managed to recover and still be first over the finish line.

## Dream Win

The New Zealand coxed eight rowing team were true amateur sportsmen. They had raised the money for their trip to Munich by holding bingo games and a raffle for a "dream kitchen". The gold medal team was expected to emerge from the professional teams of either the USA, USSR or East Germany. It was the New Zealanders, however, who won.

Another Olympic competitor made a career in the movies. This time it was a horse called Cornishman V. He carried two equestrians to gold medals and then starred in two movies.

## Stolen Victory

Rivalry between the USA and the USSR continued. The most controversial event involving the two superpowers was the basketball final. Seconds before the end of the match, there was confusion among officials. After a time-out pause, they announced there was only one second of the match to go. The match ended with the USA team celebrating a 50–49 point win. Then officials decided they had made a mistake. There should have been three seconds played after the time out. The clock was restarted and in the remaining three seconds, the Soviets scored. The USSR won by one point. This was the first time the US Olympic basketball team had ever lost a match.

## Lost Innocence

It was only a matter of time before terrorists were attracted by the enormous attention the Olympics generated. The organisers of the Munich Games were completely unprepared for such an incident. The future of the Games seemed shaky again. However, the major problems at the next Games were financial.

# 1976 | MONTREAL, CANADA

*The Games of the XXI$^{st}$ Olympiad*

| | | | | | | | ❶ | ❷ | ❸ |
|---|---|---|---|---|---|---|---|---|---|
| 1976 | Montreal | Canada | 92 | 21 | 4781 | 1247 | USSR | USA | East Germany |

Politics did continue to affect the Olympic Games in Montreal. Arguments between French-speaking and English-speaking Canadians threatened to bring the Games undone before they even started.

Ruptures in international politics led to a fall in the number of athletes attending. Earlier that year the New Zealand rugby team had toured South Africa, defying a worldwide ban on sporting contact with that country in protest of its apartheid policies. African nations wanted New Zealand excluded from the Games. The IOC refused. Twenty-two African countries objected and didn't send teams to the Games.

## The Debit Games

Like all host nations, the Canadians wanted their Games to be the best ever. Yet their plan for stupendous sporting facilities and efficient transport systems proved to be too

The Czechoslovakian cycling team left their bike wheels and spare tyres unattended and they were picked up by garbage collectors and crushed.

ambitious. They built a new Olympic stadium and although it was in use at the Games, the building wasn't entirely finished till more than 10 years later.

Another big expense was security. After Munich, there were more security staff than athletes at the Olympics. The Montreal Games made a huge loss of CAN$1 billion. The people of Montreal had to pay for much of the debt through taxes. It wasn't paid off until 1993.

## Compromise

To keep everyone happy, the Canadians had two people lighting the Olympic flame: one French-speaking, the other English-speaking; one male, the other female. As always, once the Games started, everyone forgot about the pre-Games politics and got on with enjoying them.

For once the track and field events didn't provide the star of the Olympics. This time the more gentle sport of gymnastics captured the attention of the world.

## Perfection

Gymnasts compete in several different events, performing exercises on uneven bars, balance beam, vaulting horse, and the floor. Judges award a score out of 10 taking into account how difficult each routine is and how well it is performed. In the 76-year history of Olympic gymnastics no one had ever got a score of 10 out of 10...until Nadia Comăneci came along.

Nadia was a gymnast from Romania, just 14 years old and 150 centimetres (4 foot 11 inches) tall. Spectators were spellbound as she went through her first breathtaking routine on the uneven bars. No one could believe their eyes when her score went up. It was only 1.00. An announcer had to explain that the electronic scoreboard had only space for one number before the decimal point. The highest score that could be displayed was 9.99. Nadia had in fact scored 10 out of 10. Whoever designed the scoreboard hadn't imagined that any gymnast would ever get a perfect score.

Nadia competed in five events. She received a total of seven perfect scores and five medals, three of them gold. In 1989 Nadia defected from Romania and went to live in the USA.

## Broken Dreams

Even though gymnastics is a graceful sport, it can still be dangerous. During the team event at the 1976 Olympics, Japanese gymnast Shun Fujimoto broke his kneecap in his floor exercise. He didn't want to let his team mates down, so he continued on and performed his side horse routine. Somehow he managed to score 9.5. He then went through his routine on the rings. When he jumped down to finish, he collapsed in agony and had to retire from the competition.

A more serious accident happened four years later. When Soviet champion gymnast Yelena Mukhina was in training for the next Olympics, she was still recovering from an incorrectly healed break in her leg. Her coaches insisted that she train. She slipped during a beam routine, fell on her chin and broke her neck. She was paralysed and has been in a wheelchair ever since.

## Blind Ambition

Though the US male swimmers still dominated, it was the East German female swimmers who came from nowhere to sweep the pool. They won 11 out of 13 gold medals. The American women only won one gold, the Australians none. The East German women repeated their performance in the following Games. Swimmers from other countries complained that the East Germans must have used performance enhancing drugs. The East Germans claimed their opponents were just bad losers.

When the Berlin Wall fell and the two Germanys were reunified in 1989, it was discovered that these suspicions were true. Secret police records revealed that the East German government, determined to win at any cost, had organised a program of drug-taking. Athletes who refused to take drugs were left out of the teams.

East German athletes were given very high doses of steroids. Many have developed serious health problems as a result of taking drugs. Some have died.

But in 1976, tensions between athletes from the West and athletes from Communist countries was at its height. The American swimming

"The blue pills started after the 1972 Olympics in Munich...In the 1973 season we began to get injections also. No one was sure which shots were the steroids because we were pumped full of vitamins B, C and D."

**Renate Vogel**, East German athlete

team in particular was already thinking ahead, determined to beat the East Germans at the next Olympics. In 1976, they had no idea that politics would intervene. The US swimming team would never get another chance to compete against the East Germans.

# 7 | DREAMING OF GOLD

## Santa Barbara, California, 21 March 1980

*I look at myself in the mirror. I look good. Real good. The uniform fits perfectly. It's a great style, casual but smart. It's red, white and blue, of course. Trouble is, this is the only time I'll get to wear it. I heard it on the radio this morning. It's official. The US Olympic Committee has voted in favour of President Carter's boycott of the Moscow Games. I'll just sit here a minute while it sinks in.*

*Some of the other athletes have telephoned me.*

*"There's always the next Games," one of them said. "We have to support the President. He's doing the right thing."*

*He's a younger guy. Still in his teens. He's got plenty of time. Me, my time is running out. I do support the President, but I can still feel the tears welling in my eyes.*

*This isn't the first time I've missed out on competing at the Olympics. In fact I've qualified to compete in three different Olympic Games. Each time politics has stepped in and stopped me.*

*I was born in Rhodesia. I've always been a sports nut. I've* dreamed of competing in the Olympic Games since I was nine years old. Javelin has been my specialty since my teens. I qualified for the Rhodesian Olympic team back in 1972. I even went to Munich. I moved into my apartment at the Olympic Village.

"This is it," I thought. "I'm living my dream. I'm going to compete at the Olympic Games."

Then we heard that other African countries had threatened to pull out if Rhodesia took part. It was because of the politics in Rhodesia then. There was a white minority government, which no other country in the world recognised. I wasn't interested in politics, but what did that matter? The IOC banned us. We were moved out of the Olympic Village and into an army barracks. We could stay as spectators, but that was all.

The next Olympic Games was in 1976 in Montreal. I was living in America by this time. I'd got a track scholarship at Berkeley University. I qualified for the Rhodesian team again. And this time the Games weren't that far away, just across the border. Rhodesia didn't even get an invitation to compete that time.

After that, I decided to make America my home. I love the US and I'd met an American girl. We got married. In 1977 I became a US citizen. It was one of the proudest days of my life. And guess what? It means I'm eligible to be in the US Olympic team. What's more I've never been more ready. I've won the US Championship. This was going to be my Olympics.

*You know what's really funny? Rhodesia, which is now known as Zimbabwe of course, is competing in the Olympics this time. The ban has been lifted. I'm not laughing though.*

*Some of the guys have been talking about defying the boycott. It's all very secret. They plan to compete in a sporting competition in Hungary just before the Games. They say they're going to catch buses across the border into the USSR and find their way to Moscow. They've got a route worked out. They'll compete as individuals under the Olympic flag, not as Americans. It's a crazy plan. Their passports will be cancelled. They might never be allowed back into the States again. I'd do almost anything to be in the Olympics, but I'm not prepared to give up my freedom. I'll stay here…and watch the Games on TV.*

*I'll stick by President Carter. I have to. If this country hadn't made me welcome, I'd have found myself in the Rhodesian army fighting for a cause I didn't believe in. That's the way it is. I accept that. But I think I'll just stand here in my Olympic uniform in front of the mirror for a little while longer.*

**Bruce Kennedy**, Rhodesian/US javelin thrower

Some countries who supported the boycott, such as Britain and Australia, let individual athletes decide whether they would take part in the Olympics or not. American athletes were told if they tried to go to Moscow their passports would be taken away. No US athletes defied the boycott. Many athletes like Bruce never got another chance to compete in the Games.

# 1980 | MOSCOW, USSR
## *The Games of the XXII<sup>nd</sup> Olympiad*

| | | | | | | | | ❶ | ❷ | ❸ |
|---|---|---|---|---|---|---|---|---|---|---|
| 1980 | Moscow | USSR | 80 | 21 | 4093 | 1124 | | USSR | East Germany | Bulgaria |

No one objected when the IOC announced that Moscow would host the 1980 Olympics. Tension between the USSR and the Western nations was easing. It was hoped that the Olympic Games would contribute to this process. Then, for the third time, the Soviets invaded a country just before the Games. This time it was Afghanistan. American President Jimmy Carter threatened that he would organise a boycott of the Games if the USSR didn't withdraw from Afghanistan.

> In 1981, 87 years after its formation, the first woman was invited to join the IOC. She was retired Finnish runner Pirjo Haggman.

If President Carter could persuade other countries to join his boycott, the USSR's first Olympic Games would be a disaster. It was another Cold War tactic.

The USSR didn't withdraw from Afghanistan and the IOC would not consider moving the Games to another country at such short notice. Three months before the Games were due to begin, the US Olympic Committee voted to support President Carter's

Only five sports have been included in every modern Olympics—track and field, cycling, fencing, gymnastics and swimming.

boycott. Sixty-five countries decided not to accept their invitations to the Olympics. The lowest number of nations attended the Olympics since the 1956 Games.

## The Red Games

The Soviet government was determined to show that the first Communist Games would be better than anything ever seen in the West. The Opening Ceremony included a section of the crowd which held up different coloured cards to create mosaic pictures of Russian scenes and symbols. Live pictures were beamed from two cosmonauts sending greetings from space.

When the final runner of the torch relay entered the stadium, he ran towards the cauldron which towered above the stadium. There didn't appear to be any way that he could get up to light it. Then the section of the crowd below the cauldron (who were actually soldiers) produced white boards which they fitted above their heads onto poles. This created an instant stairway which the runner climbed to light the Olympic flame.

The world was definitely impressed, but in a country where food shortages were common, the lavish Games only highlighted the poverty of ordinary people.

## In the Limelight

With the USA absent, the USSR dominated the Games, winning 80 gold medals. Athletes were frustrated, knowing many of the world's best athletes weren't present.

Two track and field events probably weren't affected by the boycott, because the world record holders were both present. Sebastian Coe held the world record for the 800 metres, while Steve Ovett was the world record holder for the 1000 metres. They were joint world record holders for the 1500 metres. The press had made much of the rivalry between these two British athletes. Spectators worldwide eagerly awaited the contest.

Everyone expected Sebastian Coe to win the 800 metres, and spectators were surprised to see him running last in the final. In his final sprint he managed to claw his way into second place. Steve Ovett won gold. Though most athletes would be pleased to win a silver medal, Sebastian was bitterly disappointed. He held the world record in the 800 metres for almost 20 years from 1979 to 1997, but he never won an Olympic gold medal in the event.

Steve Ovett was the favourite for the 1500-metre race. He had won 42 races in a row at this distance and was confident he was about to make it 43. Sebastian Coe had other ideas. Though the pair made their final acceleration at exactly the same time, Sebastian won. The British track and field team went home with five gold medals.

## Double Vision

The rowing events took place on the Krylatskoe Rowing Canal which had been specially built for the Games. When the winners of the men's coxless pairs race reached the finishing line, spectators and officials must have been rubbing their eyes. The gold medal pair were East German identical twins Jörg and Bernd Landvoigt. Three seconds later, the silver medallists rowed over the finishing line. They were another set of identical twins, Yuri and Nikolai Pimenov of the USSR.

There were more twins at the Moscow Olympics. Another set of East German twins was part of the gold medal-winning men's coxed four team. In the freestyle wrestling, Ukrainian twins won gold medals in different events.

## Soviet Success

Even though so many countries boycotted the Moscow Games, they were still successful and are remembered for spectacular ceremonies, happy atmosphere and lack of rain. Yet the Cold War had been effecting the Olympics and athletes in one way or another for four decades and its effects weren't over yet.

# 1984 LOS ANGELES, USA
*The Games of the XXIII^{rd} Olympiad*

| | | | | | | | | USA | West Germany | Romania |
|---|---|---|---|---|---|---|---|---|---|---|
| | | | | | | | | ❶ | ❷ | ❸ |

1984 Los Angeles USA  140  23  5230  1567 | USA  West Germany  Romania

After the Moscow boycott, the last place the IOC would have wanted the following Games to be was in America.

Unfortunately, they had no choice. Because of the growing cost of the Olympic Games only one city offered to be host—Los Angeles.

There was a lot of anti-Soviet feeling in America, and the USSR announced it was not safe for its athletes to go there. The Americans believed the real reason the USSR didn't attend was to get back at the US for boycotting the Moscow Games. Sixteen other Communist countries, including East Germany, supported the USSR and didn't attend. Even so, there was still a record number of countries attending the second LA Games.

## The Hamburger Games

The LA Olympic Committee had to make sure that their Games didn't make a loss. In the past the local government of the host city made the decisions and found the money to stage the Olympics. This time a private company was set up. They charged US$290 million for the television rights, produced a set of Olympic coins for people to buy as souvenirs, and found companies willing to donate money as sponsors.

The LA Opening and Closing Ceremonies were directed by David Wolper, the film producer who produced *Willy Wonka and the Chocolate Factory.*

Many people complained about having a soft drink company and a hamburger chain sponsoring the Olympics. The IOC laid down firm rules. There was to be no advertising at any Olympic venue. Sponsors' logos would not be displayed on Olympic athletes' uniforms. Athletes were not allowed to take part in advertising any products during the Games.

The last leg of the 1984 Olympic torch relay was run by the great granddaughter of Jesse Owens

## Women's Marathon

Three new track and field events for women were introduced in 1984— the 3000-metre race, the 400-metre hurdles and the marathon. It had taken sportswomen almost 100 years to convince sporting organisations that long-distance races wouldn't harm women's health.

The marathon was the most significant. Women who had previously tried to enter marathons around the world had been dragged from the track by officials and spectators. The emergence of women-only marathons had finally changed sporting officials' minds. As the lead runners entered the packed LA stadium, spectators cheered them loudly.

American Joan Benoit started running to get fit after she had broken her leg while skiing as a teenager. She continued to run and successfully qualified for the US Olympic team less than two weeks after she had knee surgery. At the LA Olympics, Joan led throughout the race. She won by almost two minutes and became the first Olympic women's marathon gold medallist.

## Rivals

Though there was no drama in the women's marathon, there was plenty in the women's 3000-metre race. A South African teenager called Zola Budd was desperate to show the world what she could do on the track. But South Africa was still banned from Olympic competition. To get around this, Zola moved to England and took out British citizenship. She would run for Great Britain instead. Zola was a shy 15-year-old who had grown up on a farm and always ran barefoot. In Britain she suddenly found herself in the media spotlight. Anti-apartheid protesters targeted sporting competitions that she took part in.

Her main rival was American Mary Decker. She was a favourite with the American crowd. Mary had overcome a number of health problems, including leg surgery because her calf muscles had grown too big for the cavities in her legs where they were supposed to fit. She was also known for occasional aggressive outbursts on the track. Spectators and TV viewers waited to see which one of the rivals would succeed.

## Collision

Halfway through the race, a tight pack of four runners led the way. Mary and Zola were among them. They were so close that Mary bumped Zola. Zola stuck out her leg to regain her balance. Mary tripped over it and fell. She pulled a hip muscle and was left writhing in pain by the side of the track. The American spectators thought Zola had tripped their hero on purpose. They started to boo her. Her leg was bleeding where Mary's spikes had dug into her leg, but the hostile crowd demoralised her. She gave up the race and came in seventh.

*Only sports that are widely practised by men in at least 75 countries and on four continents, and by women in at least 40 countries and on three continents, may be included in the program of the Games of the Olympiad.*
**Olympic Charter,** Section 52.1.1.1

That wasn't the end of the drama. Mary insisted it had been a deliberate trip. Officials disqualified Zola. Then, when they saw the video tape of the incident, they realised the incident wasn't Zola's fault at all. She was reinstated. Though they both broke world records, neither Zola or Mary competed in another Olympic Games.

## Three Firsts

The women's 400-metre hurdles was won by Nawal El Moutawakel of Morocco. Though the race was run at 2 a.m. Moroccan time, thousands of people were out in the streets celebrating her win in her home town of Casablanca. She had won Morocco's first ever Olympic gold medal. She was also the first woman from an Islamic country to win an Olympic medal. Later she became the first Islamic woman on the IOC.

## Ghetto Blaster

Paul Gonzales spent his childhood in one of the poorest areas of Los Angeles. He lived in poverty as his mother tried to provide for her eight children. The area was terrorised by warring gangs. Paul became a member of one of the gangs when he was only nine years old. By the time he was 15, he had been shot in the head and arrested for murder.

Fortunately, a policeman encouraged him to use his aggression another way. Paul started to train as a boxer. The gym where he trained was in the basement of the police station. He didn't want his gang friends to see him going into the police station, so he always climbed in through a back window. By the time he was 19 he was good enough to compete in the Olympic Games.

Paul Gonzales won the Olympic gold medal in the light flyweight division. He was also awarded a medal for the best boxer at the Olympics.

## Problem Solved

The LA Olympic organisers had come up with a solution to the problem of funding the Olympic Games. Sponsorship had proved to be an excellent way of raising money. The LA Games made a profit of US$225 million, all of which was put back into sport. Those who didn't like the idea of the Olympics being linked with multinational companies realised that there was no way to stop the Olympic Games getting bigger and bigger, and commercial sponsorship was a way to finance the Games without governments getting into debt.

*"I won this gold medal, not just for myself or my mom or my coach, but for the kids like me who are always told, "You're nothing." The only way you're going to make it come true is by dreaming it, and when you dream something, you've got to turn it into reality. Because if you don't, you just die with your dreams."*

**Paul Gonzales**, US Olympic boxer

# 1988

## SEOUL, SOUTH KOREA

*The Games of the XXIV<sup>th</sup> Olympiad*

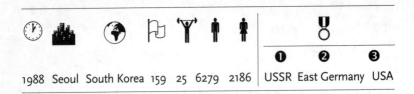

| 1988 | Seoul | South Korea | 159 | 25 | 6279 | 2186 | ❶ USSR | ❷ East Germany | ❸ USA |
|------|-------|-------------|-----|----|------|------|------|--------------|-----|

The sporting world was puzzled by the choice of Seoul for the next Olympics. Sport wasn't a big part of South Korean culture. Koreans had won six gold medals at the LA Games in judo, wrestling, boxing and archery. Before that they'd won only one gold medal in wrestling. But despite the big financial success of the LA Games, few cities around the world were willing to take on the huge responsibility of hosting an Olympic Games. The Japanese city of Nagoya was the only other contender to host the 1988 Games. Seoul won.

## The Harmony Games

Under the presidency of Juan Antonio Samaranch, the IOC was making every effort to prevent politics from spoiling the Games. After decades of international politics forcing their way into the Olympics, this IOC president was determined that the Seoul Games would be different. He spent the years leading up to the Games visiting any countries that might disrupt the Games in any way, ironing out problems and persuading governments to forget their differences. Though he was unable to win over North Korea, there were no major boycotts.

The emblem chosen for the Seoul Games was a traditional Korean design called a *samtaeguk*. It is a swirling pattern which the organisers said represented the world coming together in harmony.

The IOC also asked the Seoul organising committee to provide a new flag. The original Olympic flag which had flown at every Olympics since 1920 had become worn and faded. The new flag was made of Korean raw silk and hand sewn using traditional Korean methods. It was raised for the first time at the Opening Ceremony of the 1988 Olympics and is still in use.

## Dive Bomb

American diver Greg Louganis started his Olympic career with a silver medal in 1976 when he was just 16 years old. At the Seoul Olympics, he made everyone gasp when he performed his ninth dive in the qualifying round of the springboard event. He jumped off the diving board and completed a two and a half reverse somersault before he entered the pool. As he was completing the last turn he hit his head on the diving board. He climbed out of the pool with blood pouring from his head. But he still hadn't qualified for the

Spain's cox in the eights rowing team was only 11 years old—the youngest Olympic competitor since 1896.

finals. A doctor quickly put four stitches in Greg's head and 25 minutes later he was standing on the edge of the diving board again, ready for his next dive. It was a good dive. In fact his score was the highest of the whole qualifying round. The next day Greg won the gold medal. A few days later he also won a gold medal in the platform diving event.

## Running Rivals

Canadian Ben Johnson and American Carl Lewis had been rivals in the 100-metre race since they were teenagers. Carl had beaten Ben in the previous Olympics, but Ben was the current world record holder. The whole world was watching to see who would emerge as the fastest man in the world. Some say the 1988 men's 100-metres final was the most watched track and field race ever.

Ben Johnson broke his own world record and beat Carl Lewis by 13 hundredths of a second—which in sprint races is a big win. Canadians were thrilled. Canada hadn't won a track and field gold medal since 1932. But their celebrations didn't last long.

## Cheat

Three days later, the IOC held a press conference to announce that anabolic steroids had been found in

1985
"Drugs are both demeaning and despicable and when people are caught they should be thrown out of the sport for good...I want to be the best on my own natural ability and no drugs will pass into my body."
1989
"I want to tell [young athletes] to be honest and don't take drugs...I've been there. I know what it's like to cheat."

**Ben Johnson**,
Canadian Olympic
runner

Ben Johnson's urine sample. Ben was stripped of his gold medal and disqualified from taking part in any other events.

Anabolic steroids are made from the male hormone testosterone. When people take these drugs, it makes their muscles grow very big. When women take steroids, as well as getting bigger, stronger muscles, they also develop male characteristics such as a deep voice, facial hair and smaller breast size.

Although 42 other Olympic athletes had been disqualified for drug use since tests were introduced in 1968, Ben Johnson was the most famous. He denied that he had taken drugs at first, but then confessed he had been using steroids for seven years. One of the drugs he took was a drug injected into cows to fatten them up before being slaughtered. In his sporting career Ben won two bronze Olympic medals, but he will always be remembered as an Olympic cheat.

Carl Lewis was given the 100-metres gold medal. He won two more gold medals at Seoul and went on to win a career total of nine Olympic gold medals—a record he shares with Paavo Nurmi, Larisa Latynina and Mark Spitz.

## FloJo

Ben Johnson's disgrace grabbed the headlines and the achievements of other athletes were overshadowed by this scandal. Florence Griffith-Joyner was an American athlete who thought that looking good was as important as running well. She ran with her long hair flowing behind her and wore full makeup, including false eyelashes and

15-centimetre (six-inch) multi-coloured fingernails.

Perhaps the ghost of Baron de Coubertin would have appreciated her efforts to retain a feminine appearance as she ran. The Baron definitely wouldn't have approved of her running outfits, one of which was made of see-through lace. Newspapers called her FloJo, but she matched her fashion style with success on the track. She won gold medals in the women's 100-metre and 200-metre races at the Seoul Olympics as well as a silver and a gold as a member of the US relay teams.

When FloJo died of a heart attack at the age of just 38, some people wondered if this was the result of taking steroids.

## End of Amateurism

Anthony Nesty was the surprise winner of the men's 100-metre butterfly swimming race. When he returned home to Suriname in South America, 20 000 people (5% of the total population) welcomed him at the airport. A postage stamp and coins were issued to honour the man who is still Suriname's only Olympic medallist.

After the Seoul Olympics the Games were open to all athletes including professionals. There are only two exceptions. FIFA, the international soccer organisation, decided to limit the number of professionals allowed to play in the Olympics. Boxing is the only remaining sport in the Olympics that completely bans professionals.

Surprisingly, it was the IOC president who did the most to finally admit professionals into Olympic competition. Juan Antonio Samaranch realised it was unfair that athletes supported by governments could compete, yet athletes who supported themselves through sport couldn't. He had just one condition. No athlete was allowed to earn any money for their Olympic performance. It was the end of an era. The fight against professionalism had finally been lost. The Olympic Games would now truly be the meeting of the world's best athletes.

# 8 | LASTING THE DISTANCE

**Streets of Sarajevo, Bosnia–Herzegovina, June 1992**

*I'm running. I am out in the streets and I am running. It feels good. My family begged me to stay inside, but I came out anyway. I had to.*

*There are a few other people out on the streets—a woman with a plastic water container, a man with a child, a boy clutching three carrots. They're all running too. No one ever walks anywhere in Sarajevo. It isn't safe because of the snipers. I'm running faster than they are, though. The other people are only out on the streets because they have to be. Usually they're searching for food or filling plastic containers at one of the few places where there's still running water. I'm out here because I want to be. I'm in training. It's only five weeks till the Olympic Games. I don't know how, but somehow I'm going to get there. My event is the 3000-metre race. I can't just turn up at the Olympics and run. I have to train. That means I have to be out on these streets.*

*As I run I try to forget about the war. I pretend I'm not running through the ruins of Sarajevo, but through this city* when it was untouched by war. I remember the streets during the Winter Olympics in 1984. The cafés were bursting with people. The Zetra Arena was full of cheering crowds watching ice hockey competitions. Figure skaters swept around the rink, leaping and twirling in sequins and satin. Tourists came and admired the historic buildings, the lovely mosques.

That's what I picture as I run. But then I hear the sound of gunfire, the boom of an explosion as mortar fire destroys more of the city. Then I can't help but see the city as it is. The ruined buildings, rubble everywhere, weeds growing out of the road. I run past a ruined hotel that was full of tourists back in 1984. I pass the shattered remains of the Olympic Museum. This street is empty, apart from an old woman in black ducking from one doorway to the next…and me.

It is quiet now. As I pass one doorway I hear the sound of someone playing a violin that doesn't have all its strings. I dodge around the wreck of a burnt out car and focus again. I can do this. Things are bad but they have been worse. Last week I was prisoner in a Serbian concentration camp. I had nothing more than a slice of bread and a cup of water each day. I was sure I would die. I was lucky though. I only spent 13 days there. Then I was released in exchange for a Serbian prisoner. I can't complain. I am at home with my family now. Some days there is still not much more than bread and water to eat. But at least we can turn it into toast and tea. I am free to run. I am going to the Olympic Games in Barcelona. Somehow. No one is allowed to leave the city. I don't know how I will get past the Serbian roadblocks.

*A bullet just woke me from my daydreams. It was the sound that jolted me. My legs have turned to jelly. I'm leaning up against a wall. I can see the bullet lodged in a door frame. It missed me by no more than a few centimetres. There is a sniper out there looking at me down his gun sight. Even though he's probably a kilometre or more away, he'll be able to see me clearly. He will be lining me up in the crosshairs.*

*I dive into the doorway just as the next shot is fired. It hits the wall exactly where I was standing. The old woman in black is sheltering in the same doorway. I can hear her rasping breath. We crouch in the shadows.*

*"We must wait until nightfall," she says.*

*I shake my head. I will not be fit to run if I stay crouching in doorways. I have to train. I take a deep breath. I think about Barcelona, blue skies, green grass, happy crowds. I dash out into the street and run as fast as I can. I turn into a side street. I hope I'm out of sight of the sniper.*

**Mirsada Buric**, Bosnian Olympic runner

Mirsada did make it to the Olympic Games in Barcelona. She was escorted out of Sarajevo by United Nations personnel. She didn't win the 3000-metre race, but she did compete and her story was told all around the world.

An American man, Eric Adam, saw Mirsada training among the ruins of Sarajevo on the television news. He was so impressed by her courage that he wrote to her. They exchanged letters and Eric went to Slovenia where Mirsada was living as a refugee. He arranged for her to go to America and they were married the following year.

# 1992 | BARCELONA, SPAIN

*The Games of the XXV^th Olympiad*

| | | | | | Medals | | |
|---|---|---|---|---|---|---|---|
| | | | | | **1** | **2** | **3** |
| 1992 | Barcelona | Spain | 169 | 28 | 6659 | 2708 | Unified Team | USA | Germany |

A lot can happen in four years. A great deal happened in the world between 1988 and 1992. These world events had a big effect on the list of countries that took part in the Games. One of the events was the one that affected Mirsada—the war in Bosnia.

## New World Order

The biggest event was the collapse of the USSR, which splintered into 15 independent republics. Twelve of them competed together for the last time, calling themselves the Unified Team, marching under the Olympic flag. The Berlin Wall had fallen and the two Germanys united and sent one team to the Games for the first time since 1964. Apartheid had finally come to an end in South Africa. President Nelson Mandela was at the Games in Barcelona to watch a South African team march at the Opening Ceremony after an absence of 32 years. This time it was a multiracial team.

In gymnastics, China's Li Xiaoshuang won a gold medal in his floor routine where he performed the first ever triple backwards somersault at an Olympic Games.

The newly independent countries that had been part of the USSR couldn't raise the US$5 million needed to send the Unified Team to Spain. It looked like some of the world's best athletes would miss the Olympics again. But a group of large businesses from the West provided the money. For the first time in 20 years, every country with an Olympic committee attended the Games. There wasn't a single boycott.

## The Mediterranean Games

In the most breathtaking lighting of the Olympic flame ever, paralympic archer Antonio Rebollo shot a flaming arrow 70 metres (230 feet) through the night sky into the cauldron. The Opening Ceremony was even more spectacular than previous Games. Famous Spanish opera singers Placido Domingo, José Carreras and Montserrat Caballé sang "Barcelona", the 1992 Games theme song, written by Freddie Mercury, singer from the pop group Queen.

With the Opening Ceremony over, spectators in the stadium and TV viewers around the world settled back to watch the world's best athletes perform.

## Victorious

Jamaican-born British runner Linford Christie was 36 years old. He became the oldest man ever to win the 100-metre race. The longest standing world record was for the men's 400-metre relay race. It had been held by a US team since 1968. At the 1992 Olympics the record was finally broken—by another US team.

*"They say I am an old man and the sprint is not the old man's race. But Linford Christie doesn't believe that."*
**Linford Christie,** British Olympic runner

Russian marathon runner Valentina Yegorova came from a small village called Iziderkino. Everyone in her village wanted to see her run the race, but no one had a television set. They all contributed to buy an old black and white TV and gathered outside the Yegorova house to watch. They were thrilled when their hero won the marathon by eight seconds.

## Chinese Whispers

China, which had only returned to Olympic competition in 1984, began to make an impression on the medal tally in women's swimming. They won seven gold medals.

The muscular appearance and deep voice of 100-metre freestyle gold medallist Zhuang Yong resulted in accusations of drug use. Though Yong wasn't tested after her gold medal swim, she tested negative five days later. Yong said it was her torturous training program that had given her a muscular body. She trained for eight hours every single day of the year. Sometimes she swam fully clothed with shoes on to strengthen her swimming stroke. Her trainers didn't allow her to watch television or even visit her family.

Chinese athletic coach Ma Junren said his athletes' improvement was due to a tonic made of turtle's blood and caterpillar fungus.

## Tough Training

Fu Mingxia, another Chinese athlete, also had a cruel training program. She was taken away from her family when she was only nine years old to train as a diver. Her training including sitting on a chair with her feet on a bench and having an adult sit on her legs. This painful exercise was supposed to correct her posture. She was only 13 when she competed in the Barcelona Games. She won gold medals in both diving events.

Despite claims that Chinese athletes did not take drugs, 11 athletes tested positive in the 1996 Asian Games and four at the World Championships in 1998.

## Norwegian Wood

Olympic rowers had been using boats and oars made from lightweight fibreglass and carbon fibre since the Munich Olympics in 1972. It was a surprise, therefore, when the Norwegian quadruple sculls team competed using a rather old-fashioned wooden boat with wooden oars. This handicap made them crowd favourites and they were cheered loudly as they rowed to a silver-medal position.

## Dream Team

Now that professional athletes could compete in the Olympics, America was able to select a team of the very best basketball players from the US basketball league teams. The team included Michael Jordan, Larry Bird and Magic Johnson. It was the best basketball team ever. There was never any doubt that they would win the gold medal, but opposing teams and spectators all enjoyed the display of great basketball.

## Reconciliation

Halfway through the women's 10 000-metre race, two little-known runners emerged from the pack to pull ahead. One was white South African runner Elana Meyer. The other was Derartu Tulu, who had spent her childhood tending cattle in the Ethiopian highlands. In the last lap, Derartu pulled ahead and became the first black African woman to win a gold medal. Instead of running a lap of honour by herself, she waited at the finish line for Elana. Spectators gave the two runners a standing ovation as they embraced and then ran a lap of honour together.

In South Africa's first post-apartheid Olympics, it was a political gesture that the world welcomed.

Derartu Tulu wins
the women's 10 000-
metre race. Elana
Meyer comes
second.
(Sport the library)

# 1996 | ATLANTA, USA
## *The Games of the XXVI<sup>th</sup> Olympiad*

| 1996 | Atlanta | USA | 197 | 26 | 6806 | 3512 | USA | Germany | Russia |
|------|---------|-----|-----|----|------|------|-----|---------|--------|
|      |         |     |     |    |      |      | ❶ | ❷ | ❸ |

1996 marked the 100<sup>th</sup> Anniversary of the modern Olympic Games. Everyone was expecting that Athens would be the host, but the southern American city of Atlanta managed to convince the IOC that it would have the best venues. The Olympic Games was back in the USA for the fourth time.

## The Centennial Games

The Olympic Games just keeps growing and growing. At Atlanta the number of athletes topped 10 000 for the first time. This number was dwarfed by the 17 000 media people and the 30 000 security staff.

Perhaps remembering the pigeons that were burnt when the cauldron was lit at Seoul, at Atlanta plastic inflatable doves were released instead of the real thing.

The Olympic flame was lit by boxer Muhammad Ali, now suffering from Parkinson's disease. He was also presented with a medal to replace the one he threw in the river back in the 60s.

The Games were successful, though spectators complained about the poor public transport system and the computer system which failed several times. More seriously, a bomb went off in a park used by spectators and athletes, killing two people and injuring more than 100. The bomber was never found and no one claimed responsibility for the bombing.

## $$$

Now that professional athletes were allowed to compete in the Olympics, many of the winners were well-known. They were familiar to spectators because they had already won titles in professional competitions. They were also familiar because they often featured in television advertisements or magazine gossip columns. Andre Agassi won the gold medal in tennis. US runner Michael Johnson made headlines by winning gold medals in both the 200-metre and 400-metre races—the first athlete to do this. US athlete Carl Lewis equalled Paavo Nurmi's record of nine gold medals and won the long jump for the fourth time.

Sponsorship had become an important part of professional athletes' income. A well-known sports shoe company was paying Michael Johnson US$3 million per year to wear its shoes. The company made special computer-designed shoes for Michael. In the final of the 400-metre race he wore gold running shoes which got a lot of media attention for his sponsor.

## Almost Famous

Other athletes were breaking records and creating history, but not getting as much attention as the well-known stars. France's Marie-José Pérec matched Michael Johnson's 200-

metre, 400-metre double in the women's track and field events.

Jefferson Pérez surprised everyone by beating all the favourites and winning the gold medal in the 20 000-metre walking race. This was the first-ever Olympic medal for his country, Ecuador. His fellow Ecuadorians showered him with gifts—including a lifetime supply of yoghurt!

## Self-sacrifice

When American Kerri Strug injured her ankle during a vault in the team gymnastics event, everyone thought she would withdraw from the competition. The US gymnasts were strong contenders for the gold medal. Kerri's coach and team-mates urged her to try and do one more vault. She did, landing in a hop on her uninjured right foot. The US gymnasts won the gold medal, but Kerri's ankle injury meant that she couldn't take part in the individual events.

## Soccer Surprise

On the football field, Brazil and Argentina were the favourites. The competition started with a surprise loss by Brazil. Japan beat the Brazilian team which included soccer greats such as Ronaldo Nazario de Lima.

Nigeria didn't start well, losing to Brazil. But as the competition continued, Nigeria's form improved. The next time they were up against Brazil, Nigeria beat the soccer superstars in the final minutes of the game. To everyone's surprise, Nigeria made it to the finals. Once again, Nigeria came back from a losing position to beat Argentina in the last minutes of the game and win the gold medal.

## Comeback Kid

Another startling comeback was by Australian swimmer Kieren Perkins. He had won the 1500-metre freestyle in the 1992 Olympics, but his 1996 campaign didn't start well. In the Australian Olympic qualifying rounds, he failed to qualify for his other event, the 400-metres, and was beaten by team-mate Daniel Kowalski in the qualifier for the 1500-metres. As the fastest loser in the qualifying rounds in Atlanta, he only just squeaked into the finals by a quarter of a second.

Once in the finals, Kieren showed what he could do. Leaving the other swimmers far behind, he won the race and the gold medal.

Star-class yachtsman Hubert Raudaschl from Austria became the first person to compete in nine consecutive Olympic Games.

# 2000 SYDNEY, AUSTRALIA

## *The Games of the XXVII<sup>th</sup> Olympiad*

| | | | | | | | ❶ | ❷ | ❸ |
|---|---|---|---|---|---|---|---|---|---|
| 2000 | Sydney | Australia | 199 | 28 | 6582 | 4069 | USA | Russia | People's Republic of China |

Torchbearer Wendy Craig Duncan carries the flame underwater using a specially designed flare. (Sport the library/Steve Nutt)

For the second time, Olympic athletes had to travel all the way to Australia for the Olympic Games. US television networks were horrified when they realised that the top events happened in the middle of the night in America and delayed their telecast till prime time. Australian TV viewers, used to watching Olympic events in the middle of the night, had the pleasure of watching the competition during waking hours.

## The Green Games

The Sydney organisers promised their Games would be environmentally friendly. The Olympic Village was powered by solar energy, waste water was recycled for use in toilet flushing, and all take-away food containers and utensils were made of recyclable materials.

The Olympic flame was carried 27 000 kilometres (16 800 miles) from Olympia to Sydney. It was the longest torch relay ever. As a symbol of Aboriginal reconciliation, Aboriginal athlete Cathy Freeman was the final torchbearer.

The local fauna seemed to approve of the Green Games. Visiting athletes had close encounters with Australian wildlife. Magpies attacked mountain bike racers, snakes slithered onto the equestrian course, and two whales surfaced during a sailing event. Kookaburras and possums also made appearances. Millions of large Bogong moths were attracted by the bright lights of the Olympic Stadium and fluttered around spectators and performers at the Opening Ceremony. Helpful Australian officials issued pamphlets to visiting athletes, giving them instructions on how to deal with poisonous snakes and dive-bombing magpies.

## The Disappearing Champion

Everyone was looking forward to the women's 200-metre race. Star of the Atlanta Games, French runner Marie-José Pérec, would be racing against Australia's favourite athlete, Cathy Freeman. The showdown between the world's two fastest women never happened. Marie-José attracted the media's attention as soon as she arrived in Sydney. She stayed at a hotel instead of the Olympic Village, trained at a secret location instead of the Olympic training facilities and refused to speak to the media. Then she made a dramatic exit from the Olympics, flying out of Sydney, claiming she had received threats to her life.

Cathy Freeman, competing in a hooded bodysuit and running shoes in the colours of the Aboriginal flag, won the women's 200-metres, beating Jamaica's Lorraine Graham by 47 hundredths of a second.

## Thorpedo

In the year leading up to the Sydney Games, Australian swimmer Ian Thorpe broke 10 world records. He was under a lot of pressure to do well at his first Olympics in his home town. Swimming in a bodysuit with long sleeves and legs, he began his Olympic career with a gold medal and a world record in the men's 400-metre freestyle.

An American team had won the 4x100-metre freestyle relay at every single Olympic Games since the event was introduced in 1964. This time it was going to be different.

Just an hour after his 400-metre race, Ian Thorpe was back in the pool swimming in the men's 4x100-metre relay. Thanks to Ian's great final leg, the Australian team won, breaking the Americans' amazing winning streak.

Ian Thorpe, just 17 years old, won a total of three gold and one silver medal at the 2000 Games.

## Double Dutch

Also successful in the pool were Dutch pair Pieter van den Hoogenband and Inge de Bruijn, who both won gold medals. In fact, the swimming medals were shared around. Americans were still prominent among the medallists, Australia was too, but Italy, Sweden, Romania and Ukraine also won gold medals.

Though spectators were thrilled to watch the world's fastest swimmers in races won by just fractions of a second, they also cheered on the world's slowest swimmer.

## Eric the Eel

FINA, the international swimming federation, had a program for encouraging swimming in countries that didn't have an Olympic team. As a result, in one heat of the 100-metre freestyle, three nervous swimmers from non-swimming nations were lined up to race. The swimmers from Nigeria and Tajikistan both jumped before the starting buzzer and were disqualified.

*"The first 50 metres were okay but in the second 50 metres I got a bit worried and thought I wasn't going to make it. Then something happened—I think it was all the people getting behind me."*
**Eric Moussambani**, Equatorial Guinean Olympic swimmer

141

Eric Moussambani of Equatorial Guinea had to swim the heat alone.

Eric had only learned to swim nine months earlier and he had never swum in a 50-metre pool before. His swimming technique was terrible. During the second lap it looked like someone might have to jump in and save him. But with the crowd's encouragement he managed to finish. His was the slowest time, but spectators cheered him as they had the winner of the race. Eric, one of the slowest swimmers in world competition, made headlines internationally.

## Martial First

Though it had been a demonstration sport at two previous Olympic Games, taekwondo was an official Olympic sport for the first time at the 2000 Games.

Vietnam had been competing in the Olympic Games since 1980. At the Sydney Games, after 20 years of competition, Vietnam won its first Olympic medal. Twenty-six-year-old Tran Hieu Ngan won a silver medal in women's taekwondo.

## East Timor Four

East Timor didn't have an Olympic Committee. It was only a year since its violent transition to an independent country. The IOC wanted the world's newest nation to take part in the 2000 Olympics, so four athletes from East Timor—a boxer, a weightlifter and two marathon runners—were allowed to compete. The four athletes competed as individuals. Dressed in white they entered the stadium at the Opening Ceremony under the Olympic flag to enthusiastic applause. When East Timorese runner Aguida Amaral ran into the stadium as she completed the marathon, she was cheered almost as loudly as the winner, even though she came 43$^{rd}$ out of a field of 45 runners.

The spectators' support for Eric Moussambani and the East Timorese athletes seemed to prove that, even in an era of professionalism, the Olympic motto held true. It was still more important to take part than to win.

Beach volleyball women's final, Australia versus Brazil. The official uniform is a sport bikini. What would Baron de Coubertin have thought of that? Below, a woman plays tennis circa 1920s. A lot has changed since then. (By permission of the National Library of Australia)

# INTO THE FUTURE

In 2004 the Olympic Games will return to Athens—birthplace of the Olympics and host of the first Games of the modern era. It looks like it will be the biggest Games ever. After 108 years, the Olympic Games shows no signs of fading.

Two world wars, boycotts and terrorist attacks haven't diminished the world's enthusiasm for the Olympic Games. The TV audience for the 2004 Games is expected to be larger than the 3.7 billion people who watched the 2000 Games. When Athens organisers advertised they needed 60 000 unpaid volunteers to help stage the Games, they received more than 110 000 applications. A year before the Games were due to begin more than a million tickets to events had already been sold.

*"We pursue one ideal, that of bringing people together in peace, irrespective of race, religion and political convictions, for the benefit of mankind."*
**Juan Antonio Samaranch**,
IOC President
1980–2000

## Still the Tops

Athletes from around the world dream of becoming Olympic medallists. Even those earning millions of dollars still consider that an Olympic Gold medal is the ultimate sporting achievement.

Yet the IOC can still claim that it is more important to compete in the Olympic Games than to win. Of the 201 countries that will take part in the 2004 Games, 86 of them have never won a medal of any sort. There is still a sense of pride in just competing in the Olympic Games, even if a country can only send one or two athletes who have little chance of winning.

## Unisex

At the Sydney Olympics, two-thirds of the competing athletes were women. They competed in 24 sports including weightlifting and the modern pentathlon. These two sports had been male-only events since the beginning of the Olympic Games. Wrestling was the only sport with no female events. In Athens in 2004, female wrestling events will be introduced. It has been a long time since anyone suggested that women are too fragile to play sport.

## War Against Drugs

In 2003 new tests were developed to screen for a steroid called tetrahydrogestrinone (THG) which had previously been undetectable. British champion runner Dwain Chambers tested positive for this performance enhancing drug. There are rumours that more athletes will test positive to THG. People are wondering how many previous Olympic medals and world records were achieved by athletes taking drugs.

It seems there will always be athletes who want to win at any cost. There are those willing to cheat if they think they can get away with it, even though they know the drugs

At the 2004 Olympics, the men's and women's shotput events will be held at Olympia. It will be the first time women have ever competed at this site.

could result in serious health problems or even death. The science of drug detection will always be one step behind the science of drug development. The IOC will never catch all the cheats.

There are those who think performance-enhancing drugs should be an acceptable part of sport, just as improved running shoes and streamlined swimsuits are. Could the unthinkable happen? Just as the world got used to women and professionals taking part in the Olympic Games, could we eventually accept athletes who use performance-enhancing drugs?

## Harmony or Hatred?

Over its history, the Olympic Games has introduced athletes from all around the world to international audiences. It has given athletes from all racial backgrounds a chance to compete in international sports.

One of the IOC's goals is to make a positive contribution to world harmony. Afghanistan, banned from competing when it was under Taliban rule, has been reinstated as an Olympic nation. In 2003, just two months after conflict officially ended in Iraq, IOC delegates went to Iraq to help reform the Iraqi Olympic Committee.

The Olympic Games is a competition. Athletes from different nations race against each other, their only goal to beat everyone else. Does this really encourage peace and harmony in the world? Or do the Olympic Games encourage nationalistic pride, creating tension and rivalries between countries?

## Olympic Power

In recent years there has been criticism of the IOC, the organisation that has complete power over the Olympics. Some IOC members were sacked for accepting bribes to vote for cities bidding to be Olympic hosts. The IOC is not a democratic organisation. The current 125 members hand-pick those who will join.

It is taking a long time for the influence of Baron de Coubertin to be removed from the IOC. It took nearly a hundred years for the IOC to invite a woman to join. There are still only 11 female members. There are still a number of princes and princesses on the IOC, but 40 members are former Olympic athletes.

## Ghost of the Baron

Baron de Coubertin could never have imagined his Olympic Games would grow so big and that technology would enable billions of people to watch them. If he could see them today, he would be proud that his Olympic Games has become a truly international event showing no sign of losing its popularity. He would no doubt disapprove of all the professional athletes involved and so many women (some of them dressed only in bikinis!). But he would be pleased that after more than 100 years, the goal of the Olympic Games is the same as when it started—to bring people from all over the world together to play and watch sport in peace and harmony.

# ACKNOWLEDGMENTS

I'm not a very sporty person, but I was intrigued by the story of the Olympic Games and how it has developed over the years. I struggle to go to the gym a couple of times a week, so the dedication of the athletes was inspiring. I was also impressed by the commitment of the organisers to keep this international event going for over 100 years. The political ups and downs of the Olympics fascinated me.

The Olympic Games is a big topic to cover. In my research, the main books I referred to were:

*The Complete Book of the Summer Olympics* by David Wallechinsky

*Whitaker's Olympic Almanack: An Encyclopaedia of the Olympic Games* by Stan Greenburg

*Historical Dictionary of the Modern Olympic Movement* by John E Findling and Kimberly D Pelle

I could not have written this book without the thorough research of these authors.

The official web site of the International Olympic Committee has all the main facts and figures for every Olympic Games as well as profiles of hundreds of athletes.

It can be found at:
http://www.olympic.org

The official web site for the 2004 Games is:
http://www.athens2004.com

I found the following unofficial Olympics web sites very useful:
http://www.kiat.net/olympics
http://www98.pair.com/msmonaco/Almanac/

There are millions of web sites about the Olympic Games and Olympic athletes. Check some of them out.

Happy reading

Carole Wilkinson

# INDEX